The Art of Farting

Soon the reign of fresh air will be all over.

Parviz Shirmohammadi

Disclaimer: For Entertainment Purposes Only!

The author has written this book to entertain you and make you laugh in your free, relaxing time. After you have worked for a long day, you deserve a chance to relax, laugh, and have a great time.

By reading this book, you agree not to use the information presented here to create an incredibly malodorous harmful environment for others in any adverse manner.

You agree with the following:

1. You agree not to break gas in closed environments and social gathering places.

   Social gatherings could well include:

   a. Family parties, birthday parties, conferences, and all job-related parties.

   b. Official meetings include religious praying sessions, engagement parties, weddings, graduation ceremonies, and classroom sessions.

   c. Dates (Yes, that includes blind dates, too. Only if you were trying to relieve yourself of the company of the opposite sex. Your total stranger will indeed take a note of it. Remember that you could never get away with it.

2. Should you choose to act otherwise, you agree not to hold the author or publisher accountable and responsible for the overall consequences of your harmful malodorous actions.

3. Any other responsibility or claims made by you will be dismissed because of the nature of your smelly purposes.

4. The information here was correct at the time of publishing. However, we cannot assume any liability to any party for any damage, loss, or evident disruption caused by errors or omissions. Whether those errors or omissions result from your sole negligence, accident, or any other cause.

5. Under no circumstances will the author or the publisher accept any liabilities resulting from the harmful actions of the readers involved.

The Art of Farting / Parviz Shirmohammadi. —1st Edition.

ISBN: 978-1-7367427-0-9

Edited By: Roxana Coumans
Cover Design By: Arash Jahani
Layout By: Arash Jahani

The Art of Farting

This book SHOWS everything you always
Wanted to know about your fart.
What your biology teachers never
told you about your most basic Bodily
Function.

BY
Parviz Shirmohammadi

Written by a Man Who Has Researched,
Experienced and Suffered the Effects of
Second-hand Farting in Life

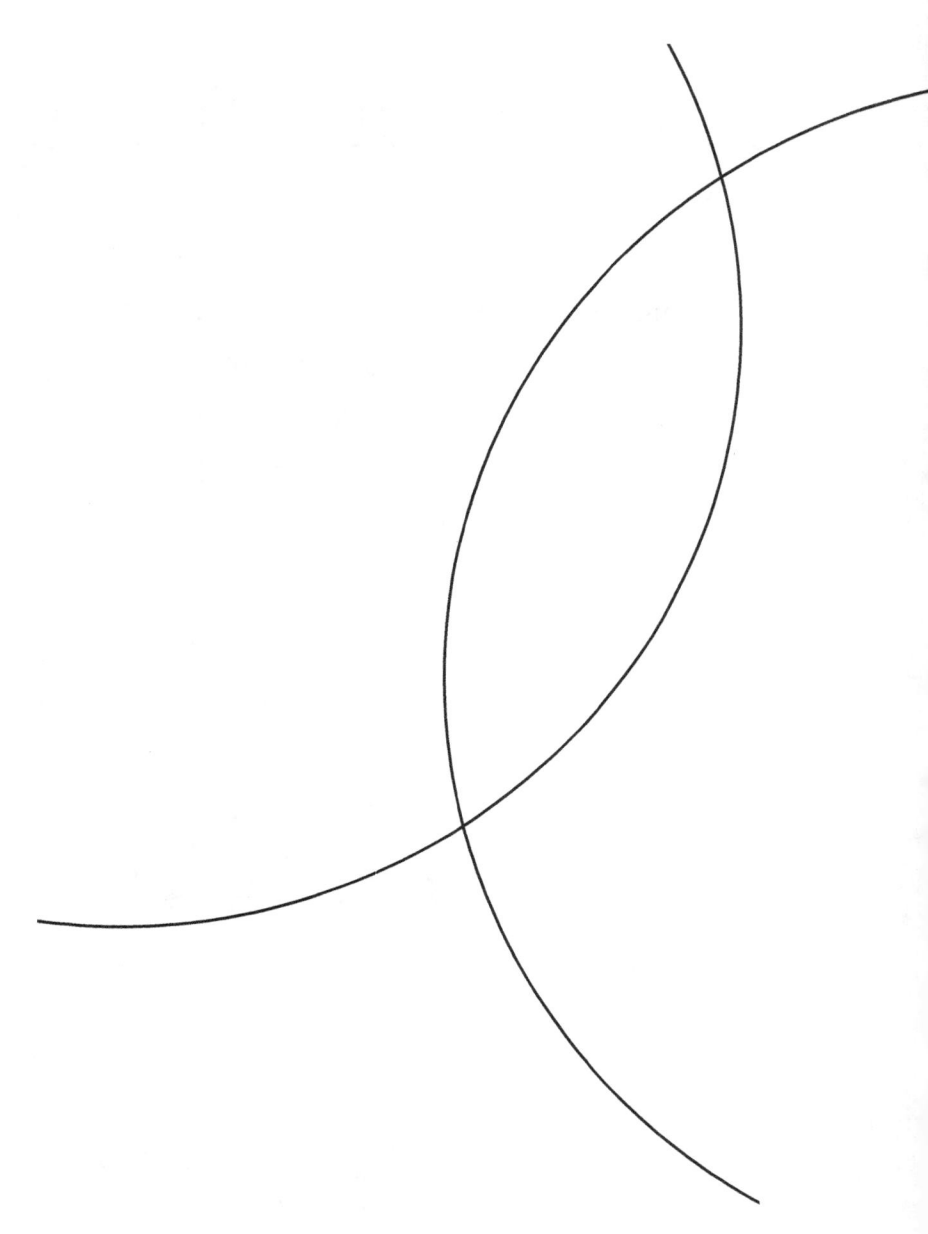

PREFACE

Why A Book about Farting?

I originally authored this book because I wanted to create an amusing and hilarious book for readers worldwide. This book guarantees you will have a shame-free future. It helps you develop the skills required to be a sound Farter so you don't become a laughingstock.

Passing gas in the right place at the right moment is enough to prevent having the most embarrassing moments of your life.

Upon authoring this book, I only had two questions on my mind. What if I could write an entertaining, funny, and hilarious book that could make readers happy all the time? What if I could create a hilarious and entertaining book that leaves the best and funniest reading experience for all readers?

You know this is the type of book that could make any reader laugh and create an enjoyable experience. It took me a day to mentally organize that idea.

On the same day, I had a precise writing action plan for the whole general mapping of this book on my mind. The fact is comedy books are tough to write.

It is hard to develop a hilarious idea and a totally different complicated viewpoint and turn it into a funny book. The other complex challenge is how different parts of the world have different views about a specific hilarious idea.

However, I am glad that I wrote this book. I had the best time of my life writing this book. Every single creative, and funny sentence that I wrote, made me extremely happy.

I thought if it could make me a much happier person, it would make any reader in this world much more euphoric, too.

After all, who wouldn't want to read a comedy book, relax, laugh, and have a great time? If you're going to laugh and relax after returning home from work, this is the book that you would want to read.

It is easy and clear to understand and read. Thus, all readers at any level can enjoy reading it.

It does not matter who you are or where you live in this world. Laughter always helps you recharge, energize your strength, and be ready for the upcoming career and life challenges that lie ahead. If my humorous book makes you laugh out loud and roll on the floor, then I have done my best writing job for you.

Happy Reading!
Parviz

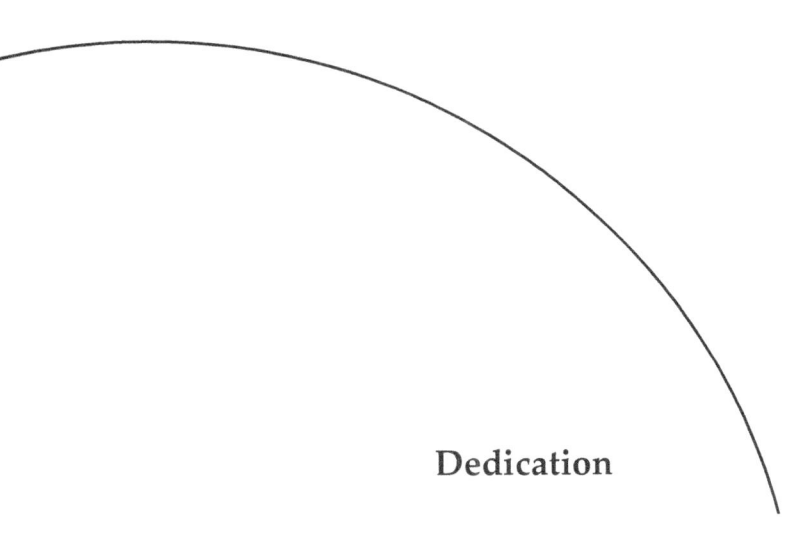

Dedication

I am dedicating this book to my dear parents, especially my beloved late father (Enayat), who created a great household where laughter, creativity, kindness, and love were always present and welcomed. He always believed in me and my writing talents far more than anybody else. He will be missed in my heart forever.

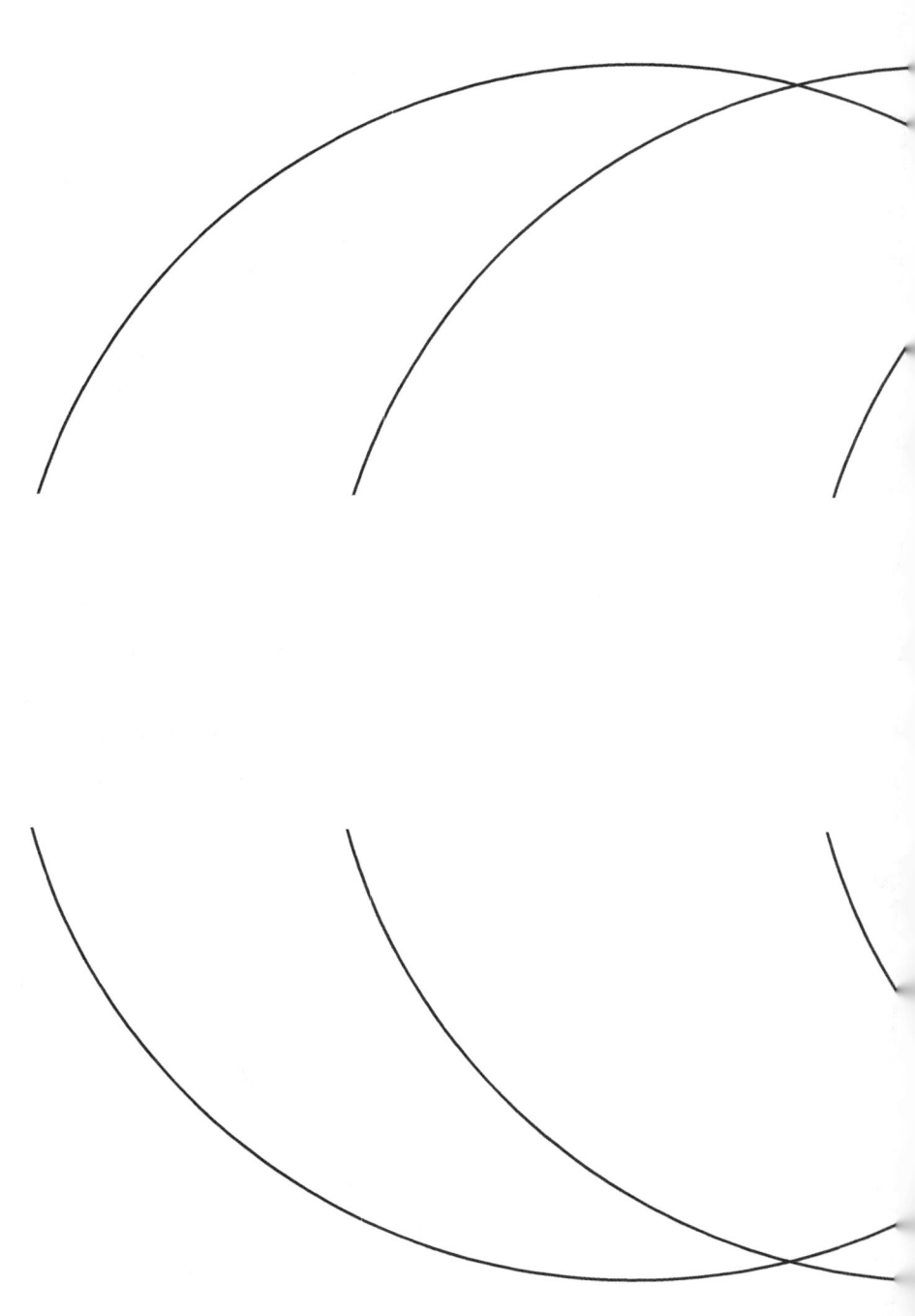

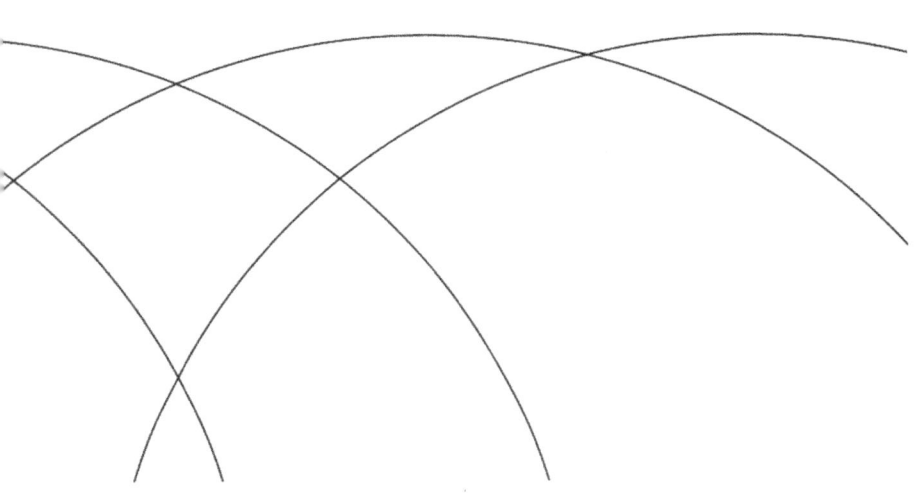

Humans Perform The Act of Farting Daily.

I just wrote a book about it.

Parviz

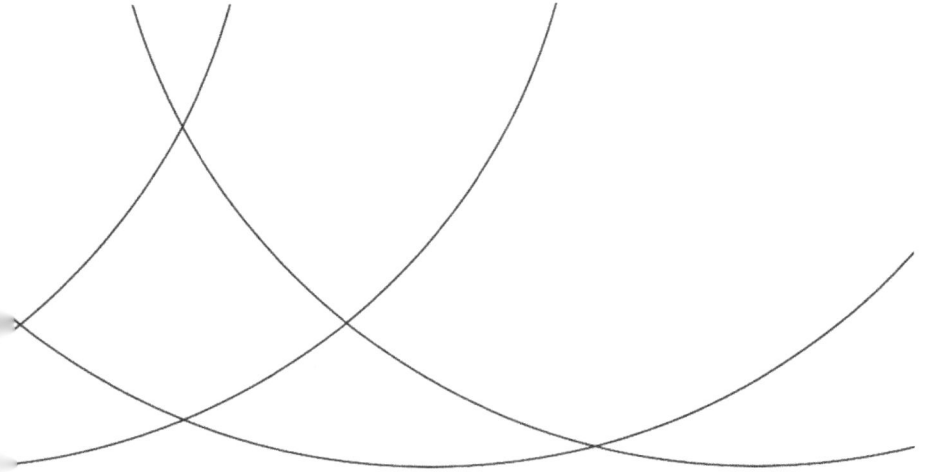

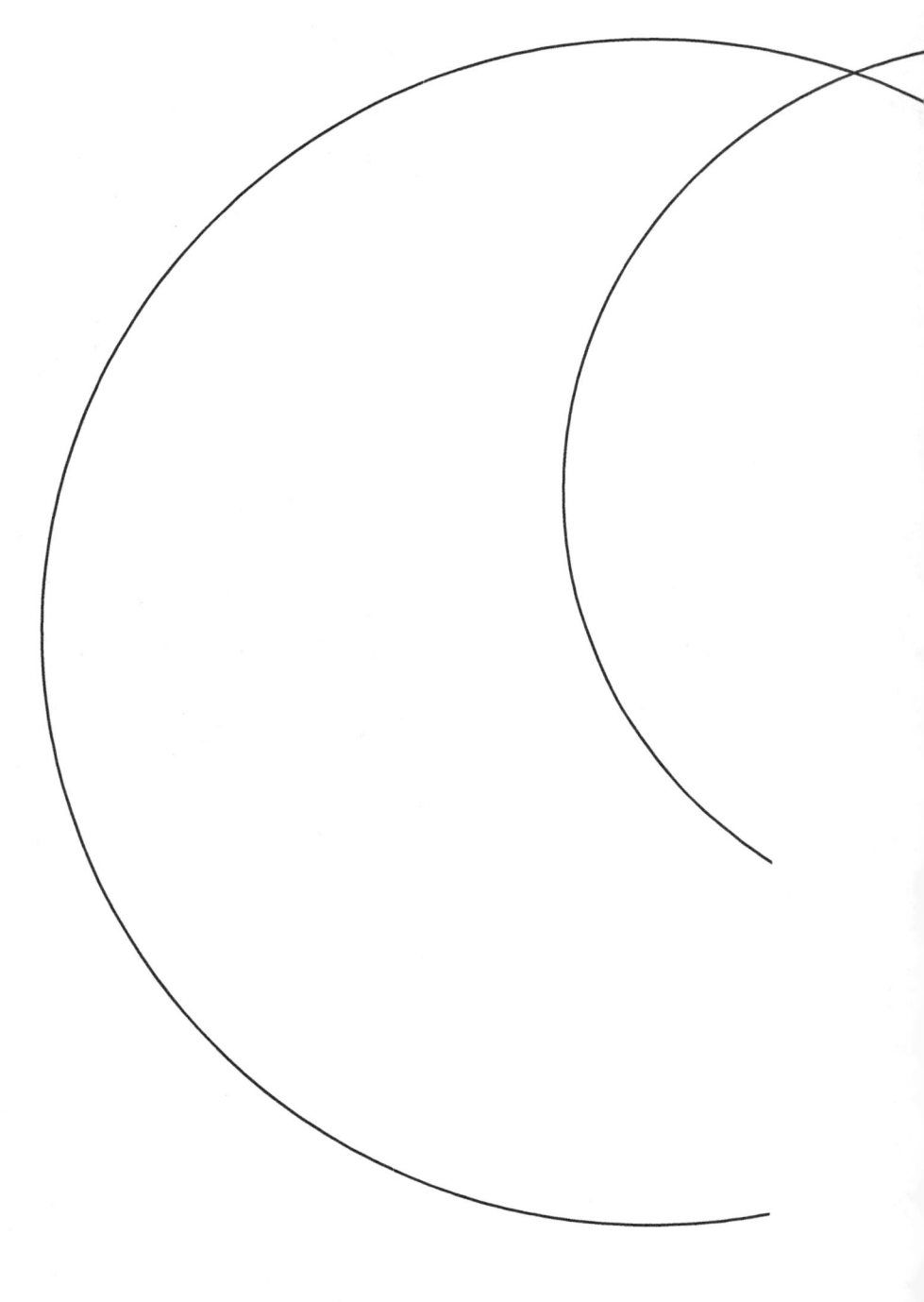

Contents

ACKNOWLEDGEMENTS

First and foremost, I would like to thank my dear brother Payam who has always supported me in writing and publishing this comedy book from the very beginning. He has been my number one supporter in all my writing projects. He has been kind enough to listen to my different funny ideas to make this humorous book far better than before. He has a heavenly talent to listen carefully and patiently to what I came up with for this book and provide the best and most effective critical outlook on them.

I would like to thank all my other family members, relatives for their patience and support, co-workers, and new friends discovered during this work's writing and publishing.

Furthermore, my sincere heartfelt appreciation and gratitude go to my dear friend Mr. Michael Yong Lee. He has the genuine spirit of the late legendary Bruce Lee in him. Sometimes in life, to achieve your dreams and reach your goals, you need someone who believes in you and encourages you daily. Thank you for being there for me. I will never forget your kindness. It is such a great privilege to know you and have you as a friend. Thank you very much for believing in me. You will always have my most tremendous respect, care, attention, and love.

Writing and entertaining readers worldwide are all the best parts of my life.

I could not write this book without the ongoing moral support from all the people mentioned earlier.

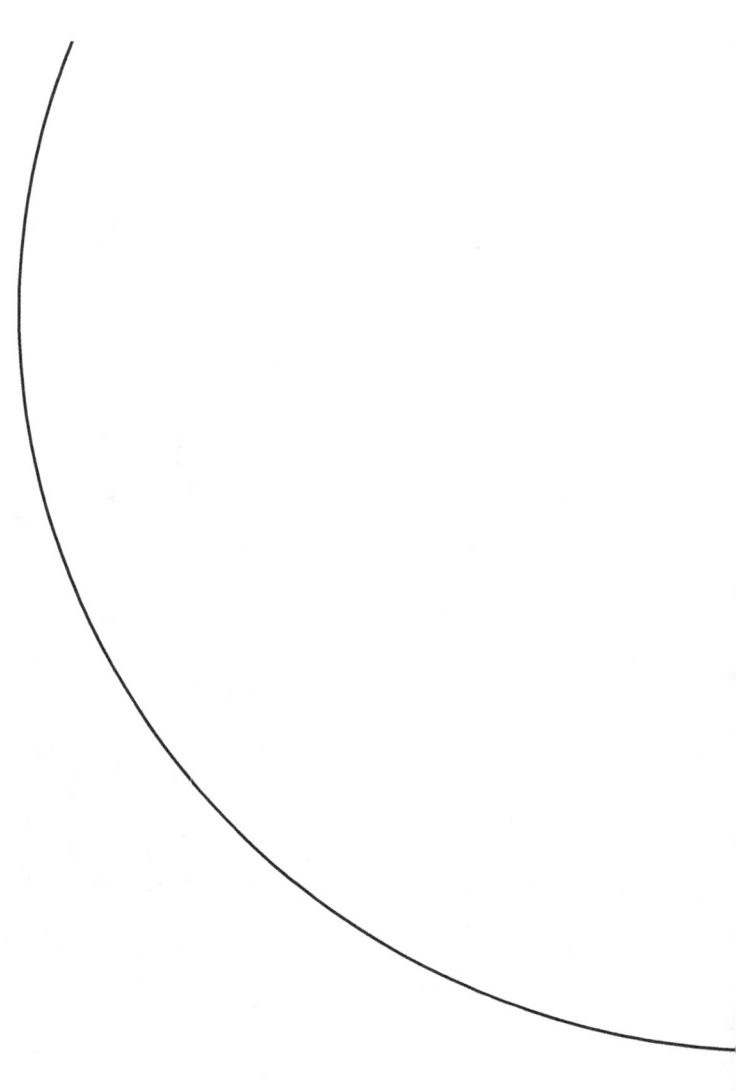

CHAPTER 1

The History of Farting

When it comes to the concept of farting, you may think that there is no clear history about it anywhere. However, there has always been a great deal of historical information about farting throughout the different times. And make no mistake, the various governments have tried to keep it as one of their most guarded secrets from the public.

They had a compelling reason. All government entities believed that if people got a chance to experience the real power of their farts. They would easily use it to overthrow the government.

In ancient Rome, the Senate Members tried their best to ensure no ordinary people had access to their secret Underground Windbreaker Society.

The UWS membership rule was simple and easy to understand. No member could break gas in public loudly. That went to explain why all members were releasing gas only in underground areas. And why were they doing their gas-passing ritual underground? There were convincing reasons. First, think about it for a second! How could they do it over the ground?

Second, the other reason was that no one complained about exposing people to the evil effects of farting in the unground areas. If the public complained about the bad smell, they could blame the person using the bathroom.

In ancient Persia, any time that the Persian army wanted to disarm the enemy without having bloodshed. They would use their unique secret weapon, the destructive malodorous power of their farts.

They would do it uniquely. The prepared soldiers would go to a top height, remove their pants and underwear, bend down and break gas right along the direction of the wind blowing. The rest of the military operation was easy, and most of the time, it would proceed automatically.

The enemy had no choice but to get exposed to the incredibly foul-smelling massive cloud of thousands of farts.

Moments later, all of them would fall to the ground and pass out for hours. An unconscious enemy is always a weak one.

By then, it was not hard to remove their weapons and tie up their hands. The Persian Army captured and conquered so many lands that way.

It is said that the Great Alexander discovered the ancient secret to create far better, deadlier human gas. He was the only one who secretly watched the significant Zeus's flatulence rituals from his hideout.

The Gods were always one step ahead of everything humans were good at performing. Flatulence power was among the essential skills that they excelled in doing all the time.

Later, at any time, Alexander and his army were outnumbered by the enemies. Alexander would lead the entire army to the most apparent victory using his smelly farts far sooner than anybody else.

He could release one right at the beginning of his attack. The enemies' horses and even elephants could sense his gross gas from a mile away. He would neutralize them and make them fall to the ground while their riders were on their back.

That removed the mightiest parts of their army first and foremost. He would proceed and fart away all around the enemy forces from then on while riding his black horse swiftly in spiral riding movements. That effective milestone move was the basis of all his victories worldwide.

He always fought along with his most skilled windbreakers riding behind him. He used his effective silent Fart as his most secretive chemical weapon against all his foes.

Many countries decided not to even go to war with him as soon as they found out the truth behind all his glorious victories one after another.

However, humans learned that if they could fart on an animal's face. Then, they could show their real fart power. Soon, the animal world noticed they could never defeat humans who had deadly farts in their bottoms.

Overall, the flatulence power guaranteed protection against invasion, pillaging, manslaughter, and more.

CHAPTER 2

The Protective Role of a Fart

A single fart travels at a speed of over 40 feet per second. That is far slower than the speed of sound. However, the gross fatal effect of that velocity is absolute. The fresh air just ceases to exist instantly.

In recent years, many international archeologists discovered numerous caveman paintings that proved and illustrated how troglodytes were using the power of their gross smelling farts to defend themselves.

The latest research findings proved the elusive controversial history of wind-breaking dates back to the earliest cavemen and cavewomen times. Scientists have discovered caves worldwide, showing charcoal paintings proving how cave dwellers were using the malodorous power of a fart to survive.

Archeologists can quickly show that primitive humans were using windbreaker power to defend their reigns.

In the animal kingdom, almost all-powerful animals use urination to mark their territory.

They found many paintings that showed how primitive humans caught the wild animals using humanly made giant stone traps. The whole process was self-explanatory and easy to do.

First, the assigned potent cavemen would attack the leader animal of their herds. They would lure the angry animal into the web, mostly a large crack in the mountains.

At the same time, many other people were already standing on top of the trap. They were all roped to big nails. It was fatal to fall into the trap. Even if they could survive the fight with the angry animal, soon, they would be dead in case of exposure to the massive cloud of farts.

Let us think about it for a second! In those days, there were no emergency systems like 911. It was not like they could take out a cellphone and call it in and say: "Hello, 911, a person just fell down the trap and is seriously suffocating very badly."

Later, as soon as they could see, the animal was in it, and once they were sure, it could not escape.

Then the cavemen would quickly turn around and point their butts down towards the animal. Then they would all release their most significant and loudest farts over the entire area of the stone cage simultaneously. A big remarkable loud bang echoed all through the mountain. It was so loud and scary that other animals were peeing everywhere while running away.

That would create a stinking cloud of foul human gas. The trapped animal had no way to fight back or even harm any of the humans. The poor animal could not even climb the cliffs to reach them and hurt them in any way.

They were witnessing how the animal's face was changing colors and was looking extremely pale. The animal was opening its eyes and was happy to find out it was still alive. Then, it would lose its conscience completely, and after a few hours, the wind would take away all that gas.

That was the source of hilarious fun and laughter for them. The amused cave people were all pointing their fingers towards the captured animals while laughing their butts off.

The cavemen would then release the exposed animal into the wild. Then, since the free animal was the toughest one in their herd, it would look feeble and defeated by the mere human farts upon returning to its reign. The cavemen repeated this awful gassy procedure for as many wild animals as they could get their hands on.

That was the first time in which humans experienced the remarkable power of teamwork with the highest magnitude.

Soon, cave-dwellers started to use their trained buttocks as their ongoing available arsenal. The primary tool of their artillery was their most potent and stinking farts.

They also started training their bodies to be fully capable of long-range indirect fire at a target too distant from them. Many days they went to the top of the mountains and started effective remote target practice.

They would release gas facing the wind's direction while targeting the distant animal's face with their butts.

Although, the entire process proved to be useful most of the time, failures were bound to happen. Sometimes, they would precisely aim for the animal's head, but their farts would accidentally land on the animal's behind. That was extremely disappointing and discouraging for the responsible gas-releasing party.

After all, hitting the animal's face could have been one of the most effective ways to make the animal fall and hit the ground.

Later, they discovered they had no control over the intensity of the wind blowing in different directions.

Some more intelligent species, including wolves, chimpanzees, and foxes, started to counter-attack human bodily weapons with their gas.

That stone-age targeting system created the idea of building and designing the first biological warfare weapons of mass destruction.

In today's world, what you see in modern chemical warfare is genuinely the result of human societies' experience who dared to use all their flatulence abilities strategically.

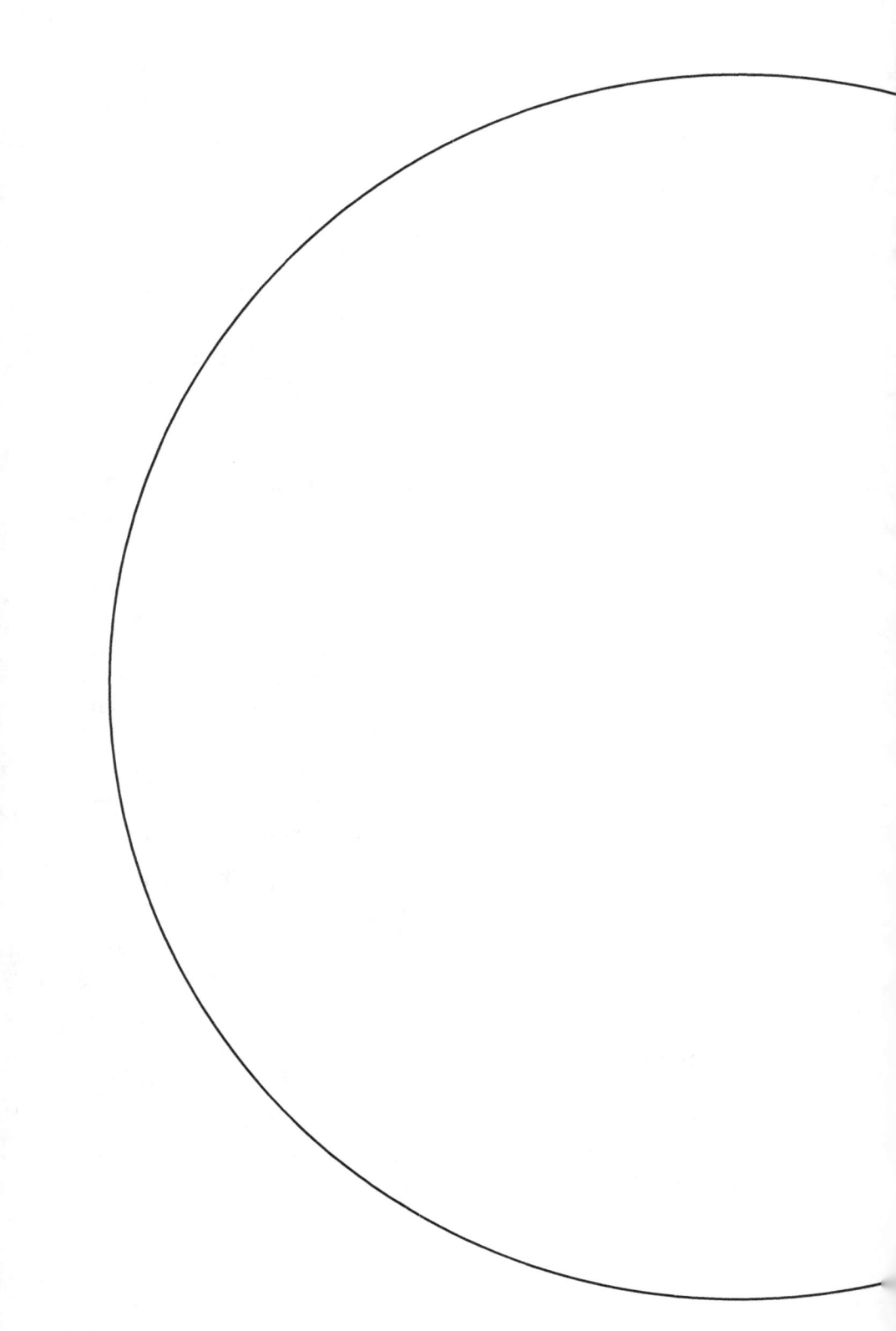

CHAPTER 3

The Legend of King Fartan

Most people can perform simple research about the greatest farters throughout history. The long list includes Genghis Khan, Pharaoh of Egypt, Adolf Hitler, Alexander the great, And Darius the Persian King.

However, you can never find the story of the first ancestor and pioneer of the entire great farters. Who was the first historical greatest Farter?

It is time to hear about a great King who was the first historical ultimate Farter. His name was Fartan. He was the leading mystical man who held the key to all upcoming farters around the globe.

Since the dawn of creation, in the vast land of Fartista, humans had found out that they needed adequate protection and strong defense against all dangers in the world to survive.

Soon, they started learning all the necessary skills to fight off animals and other humans attacking them during various times of the year. However, they learned how to train their bodies at a very young age to get tough and be far much more potent all the time.

They also looked for other types of skills that they could use for protection.

Gradually, they set up many weekly physical contests among strong men to choose and find the most muscular man who could lead them to victory on the battlefields.

They were required to temporarily knock out their opponents by any physical means possible to win. Then, one day, a new young fighter decided to use all his bodily powers to win any matches.

People later called him: Fartan. Soon the world would know how Fartan was the only man who dearly believed in the hidden power of a gross fart. He thought for days to come up with a highly effective winning idea.

One day while Fartan was watching a fight between two horses. He noticed the more petite horse used the power of his smelly gas to confuse the much bigger horse.

The more miniature horse performed an unusual fighting technic to defeat his opponent quickly. It was an instant combination of fast kicks to the neck and swift delivery of the Fart. Nobody had used it before.

Soon the other horse would fall to the ground. It would instantly receive the released gas all over its face. Moments later, the defeated horse would lose the ability to breathe the fresh air, and soon it would become unconscious.

Fartan whispered: "Wow, that is indeed very interesting. Now, if only I could find a way to save my best farts, knock down my rival to the ground, point my butt towards his face and release my most grossFart all over his face. Victory shall be mine forever."

Fartan memorized and practiced all the sneaky moves and how effectively to pass his most unpleasant Fart all over his opponent's face. He secretly tried eating many different types of foods.

He went to the forest for many nights, passing gas in the open air and smelling his farts to create the best and most potent Fart.

Boiled eggs, red beans, cabbage, and spicy foods made more farts containing the most unpleasant odors. Fartan still needed to learn how to release the most pungent gas at the precise, effective moment. That sparked an exciting motivation in him.

He finally invented his rare fighting fart after five tedious months. He was now ready to use his hidden biological weapon. Nobody else had it. He called it the victorious odor.

He started his restless training. He tried to create and master a technique to leave his opponent partially paralyzed during the fight.

He thought: "What if I could target any rival's face from afar with my bottom? But then again, if I fart loudly during the match, the judges immediately consider it an illegal move, and I will be disqualified from all sporting events forever. I have to be very careful. I must find another way to do it."

Then he tried using his several farts to knock down various objects such as empty bottles, branches, and even small pumpkins from a distance.

He placed a wooden log 100 yards away. Then, he set a row of empty terracotta bottles with a specific enough room among them. To make his target practice more effective, he decided to have at least 80 inches of space among all bottles.

His ultimate goal was to succeed at pinpointing the head of any opponent from a distance and hitting it with his Fart.

So, late at night, while everyone else was sleeping at home. He was going to an open-wide closest forest performing his target practice. He knew well if anyone else found out about his secret training, they will use it against him someday.

Fartan turned around, removed his pants and underwear. He tried to target each bottle separately with his butt. He released his first significant gas while targeting the first bottle. A loud noise went throughout the whole forest. However, he had absolute peace of mind. The forest was at least three miles away from his town. People could not hear anything from that far away.

He heard a big thump. It seemed that the bottle hit the ground hard. It was as if it fell from high altitudes in the sky.

He thought: "what happened? Did I hit it? I got to check it out."

He pulled up his underwear and pants, turned around, and ran towards the target row. To his shocking surprise, the first bottle remained upright. However, when he looked closer. He found a body of a big black bat lying close to the bottle's row. He placed the palm of his right hand over the bat's chest. The animal was still alive and breathing. It got just paralyzed for a few minutes.

He said: "Oh, God! Sorry if I accidentally targeted your head instead of the first bottle. I didn't mean to hurt you. I'm glad your head was strong enough to deal with my gross fast Fart. You're going to make it. Why are you flying right over here and so close to my farting target field, anyway? Darn it! I got to think about flying bats at night, too."

He thought: "Ok, I got it now. I must create an aerial boundary for all flying night creatures right before I start my target practice."

The next day, he went to the local market and bought four sacks of construction gypsum. He emptied all the sacks one by one at night and poured them around his target practice field. There was a clear whitish circle-shaped long line all around the area.

He was wearing a black cloth mask. He then bent over, targeted the sky with his butt, and farted in different spots along the line. That created a temporary huge smelly gas cloud in the air. It was the only way to make sure no flying animal would enter the field.

He sighed and whispered to himself: "Oh, what a relief! I finally did it. Ok, go ahead now! Go start doing your practice!"

This time he was way more focused than any other time before. He turned around, easily bent over, pinpointed and targeted the first bottle with his buttock, and looked at the bottle from right below his butt.

He let out his fastest and strongest Fart. Within seconds, the bottle got hit and was thrown away behind the target row.

He was so happy and excited about his new gross accomplishment.

He said: "Oh, yes! I did it. It worked." He jumped up and down with sheer excitement. He felt the sense of true happiness captured all his existence.

That night, he continued more target practice and knocked down all the targets successfully one by one.

Then he suddenly remembered another big issue that he still needed to figure out to use his new farting skills during any match.

He thought: "Ok, I now can easily use my Fart and my butt to hit any target from any distance. But I must get butt-naked to do it. How am I supposed to get naked in a match? They will ban me from being in public. I will be imprisoned if that happens, too. I must fix that. Think about it! You know you could find a way to get it done."

He sank into deep thoughts. He visualized different ways of solving the issue. Then all of a sudden, he remembered when poor people show up in public places wearing old torn clothes. Nobody else would even bother to mind the part of their skin visible through the torn part of their clothes.

For a moment, he felt pressure and a weight of sadness all over his heart.

He thought: "As soon as I win some money from any match. I'll try to buy clothes for poor people who can never afford to buy them. That should make them happy again."

All he needed was to have a hole in both his pants and underwear aligned precisely with his anus. That way, he could use his Fart and his butt to target and hit anyone's head during the match.

He found a professional maid who was also a skilled female seamstress. Her name was Bella. He told her that he needed to build a pea-sized hole in all his pants and underwear.

Bella was surprised and laughed: "Tell me something! Why would you want to have two holes both in your pants and your underwear? And you said they must be lined up with your orifice, too. I don't get it at all. Don't you take them off to pee whenever you are using the bathroom?"

He smiled and said: "Yes, I know how that sounds. I am not going to use them for peeing in the bathroom at all. I need them for my personal sporting goals. They will help me to be a much better fighter. That's all I can tell you now. Look, I'll even pay you extra money for all your hard work if you can do that for all my sporting pants and underwear."

She needed to create numerous rounded sewn holes with intricate detailing.

Then, to make sure she made the hole to Fartan's satisfaction, Bella asked him to try his first pants and underwear right there at her home and practice farting while wearing them.

She lit up a candle and asked him to try to put off the candle's flame just by using his Fart.

"Come on, Fartan! Go ahead! Show me what you can do with your gross secret weapon!" She said.

"This is not what I had in mind doing in your place, ok? Are you sure it's ok to stink your whole room with my stinky Fart?" He responded.

"Are you afraid of anything? What is it? Do you think I fart out rosemary and flower's scent all the time? Trust me when I fart. It is so bad. Some people would even get ready to move to somewhere else in this town. I mean anywhere but close to my home." She smirked.

"Ok, relax! I'll do it! I was just making sure I wouldn't hurt you in any way." He responded.

He turned around, bent over, made sure he lined up both holes in his clothes with his butthole. Then, he targeted the exact spot of the flame over the candle and let out his best swift Fart.

The flame went off quickly, without making the candle shake and falling from the kitchen counter.

Bella got very excited and yelled: "Yes, you did it. I knew it."

She took him in her arms, they kissed, and they both got very excited and released gas simultaneously.

"This is the best romantic moment of my life. I have never met and been with a man who could harmonize his gas with mine very carefully." She smiled.

"Remember, this is a secret between us." He asked.

"Oh, of course! Like you even have to ask," she said.

"You know something, Fartan? Sometimes, your whole life comes down to an effortless choice. Are you not excited to use the power of your gas to win all your sporting contests easily?" She said.

"Yes, of course, I am. What kind of question is that?" He responded.

"Ok, Bella! Thank you for all your help! Here is your pay. I need to go home." He said.

"Thank you, Fartan! You're a decent man." She smiled.

Fartan went back home. It was late at night. He looked up and saw the whole moon in all its glorious shape. The moonlight made the night bleaker than all the other nights. He slowly released a small silent odorless fart in the street. He was happy he was getting closer to his winning. He was thinking about Bella and how she eagerly helped him to believe in his stinky power.

The next day, he went to sign up for the entire series of all wrestling contests. Then on Saturday morning, he showed up for his competition.

Fartan looked at his opponent. This time he was fighting with a man more significant and much more potent than him. The man looked more like a beefed-up Rhinoceros. People thought he was the Rhino standing on his feet before crushing anyone on his way.

"Hey, Fartan! Look at the size of that guy! He's going to eat you alive! Son, don't fight him! Are you crazy? Cancel your fight! Live today and fight someone your size tomorrow!" the old man said.

"Old man, you worry too much. I'm not scared of him. I am well-prepared to fight him. I trained my mind and my entire body for this match. Just make sure you and your friends bet on me, not him. Ok, old man?" he answered.

They hit the big drums. The haunting loud sound of the drumrolls grabbed the instant attention of all spectators. The Judges called up both contestants.

"People of Fartista! Welcome to our first Inter-City championship match between the undefeated Rhino Man, the biggest man from the green forest city, and our own local all-time winner champion: Fartan!" The sports announcer yelled.

"This is the match we have all been waiting to see. Remember whoever wins today will be the new leader of the Fartistan army!" He said.

"Say goodbye to your people, Fartan! This game is the end of your reign. I will crush you like a bug." Rhino yelled.

"Oh, really? I think for a big guy, you also have a huge dirty mouth. I'll make sure you go back to your forest in just one piece today." Fartan calmly smirked.

"On your mark, ready, get set, and go!" The young announcer shouted out.

They approached each other. Fartan punched Rhino in his stomach as hard as he could. The impact was so hard that he farted. People screamed and laughed. Alas, it was not strong enough to make him fall on the ground.

"Damn, I guess he really is a big bad animal. Now, what?" He thought.

"Is that all you got, you little city boy? You made me fart. Don't tell me that's how you always win your fights!" He laughed loudly.

Then he punched the Fantan's chin with a swift move of his right fist. Fartan flew away through the air backward and hit the ground. He suddenly flashed back in his mind to the battle of the horses. He needed a chance to use his secret weapon.

"Get up, son! Make him fall to the ground, or you won't stay alive to win today!" The old man yelled.

Fartan got up. He started doing different complex regular exercises while he was running away from the prominent opponent's hands. The big guy got very tired of running after him. Unable to hit him even once, he paused and stood still for a moment to catch his breath.

"I have to take away his eyesight! Then I can easily defeat him." He thought.

Fartan moved back away from him quickly for a few yards, turned around, bent over, and targeted Rhino's left eye with his butt. He lined up his butthole with the other two hidden holes in his underwear and pants. He quickly released two of his fastest and most potent silent farts one after another.

To the people's shocking surprise, Rhino smashed his left eye with the palm of his right hand and yelled: "My left eye! I don't see anything with my left eye."

He turned around to find Fartan and punch him again. However, Fartan performed the same move on his right eye, too. This time Rhino went completely blind.

Moments later, Fartan jumped through the air and hit the left side of Rhino's neck with his right leg. He collapsed to the ground with a big loud thump. Then Fartan started circling him and quickly farting all over his body. He went completely numb for the remaining match. The referee waited, standing over him to see if he could still get up and fight back. He was not even able to move his fingers.

"Ladies and gentlemen, we have a winner. The winner is Fartan. He will be the new leader of our army." The referee announced loudly.

The crowd went crazy. The Fartistans were never more satisfied and excited with the final competition's results.

They yelled, "All hail Fartan! The new leader and the best champion of Fartista!"

Fartan was so pleased. He saw Bella among the crowd of people smiling at him. She was jumping up and down out of sheer happiness of his victory.

She waved her hands for him. Then she kissed her right palm and threw away a sexy coyishly kiss towards him. He pretended to catch it up in the air with his right hand and place it on his lips. He then went on to make out with his palm, passionately.

People started laughing. Fartan turned around. He realized that Rhino was still lying on the ground inside the ring right behind him.

"Oh, no! Why is he still unconscious? I went too far on him." He whispered.

He quickly looked for the two closest beautiful women in the crowd and asked them to bring a bucket of water to help Rhino get back on his feet again.

"Why are you only asking beautiful ladies to help him out, Fartan?" The referee asked.

"Well, if he wakes up and sees two other ugly men right above his head, he's going to get so angry and beat us all up. Trust me! You don't want that to happen to our people, do you? Besides, he doesn't look like a man who would hurt any beautiful woman." He responded.

"Oh, yeah! I see your point. You're so smart, man." He said.

The women brought a whole bucket of water, sat on both sides of Rhino's head. They started wetting their palms with the cold water and rubbing them all over his face. He slowly opened his eyes. He was shocked to see two lovely sexy beautiful women next to his face.

"Hey, what's going on here? Am I dead? Is this heaven?" he asked.

"No, you are not dead, you big buffoon. Come on, big guy! Shake it off! The show is over. Let's go! I'm buying you and these two lovely ladies lunch today." Fartan said.

"But I called you many bad things in front of the whole city. Are you sure you still want to invite me for lunch?" He asked.

"Look! Yes, we are rivals inside the ring, but outside the ring, we are just two people trying to get along and be friends." He answered.

"Ok, then. Let's go, my new friend!" Rhino smiled.

"Bella, come here, please!" He shouted.

Bella quickly joined them, and she took them to one of the best restaurants in town. Fartan ordered the roasted chicken, fruit salads, and beefsteak for everyone.

"Oh, Fartan! It's so good to see you here. You have honored us with your presence. Our champion is always welcome here. Welcome to my restaurant!" The old man said.

"Hey, I know you! You're the man who helped me win today. I never got a chance to say thank you. The honor is all mine, my friend. I had no idea you owned the finest restaurant in town." He said.

"I know you are so busy taking care of your customers. But, come join us when you have a chance!" He said.

"I'll see what I can do. Enjoy the food!" The old man walked away.

"Alright, everyone! Let's eat and have fun together! Let's also make sure our big guest, the man from the green forest, has the best time here in our city!" He said.

Bella sat right beside Fartan. The two lovely ladies sat on both sides of the big guy from the forest. They all laughed and started eating the fresh, delicious food. Fartan poured water in a glass, grabbed a plate, cut some chicken and steak slices, and offered them both to Bella.

"Wow, you are such a kind gentleman, Fartan! Thank you so much." Bella said.

"You are so welcome." He said.

"Oh, you are so nice to all beautiful women. I now see why all women are so good to you." Rhino said.

"So, why is that a bad thing in your mind? There must be lots of good, beautiful women in your green forest. Am I right? So, what's your real name, my friend? I don't like to call you big guy or even Rhino all the time, you know." He said.

"My real name is Triden. But once, I had to fight a massive male angry Rhino who was always releasing the most disgusting gas all around the forest every day. That big stinky animal almost made all the humans suffocate and disgusted with his routine passing gas all the time." He said.

"So, what did you do to him? Did you kill him?" Fartan asked.

"No, then, one day, I just couldn't take it anymore. I confronted him, and as soon as he attacked me with his giant unicorn. I quickly moved aside and punched the top of his head with my right fist. He lost consciousness for a few hours. Then, I tied up all his four legs and started farting over his face once every 6 hours. I also asked other people to perform the same act on him on different days. He didn't die, but I made sure he learned his stinky lesson in the most disgusting way possible. Of course, I would feed him and make sure he was not drowning in his shit for three days in a row. When I released him, he went so far away that nobody ever saw him again for the next ten years. Then some silly little kids started calling me Rhino." He said.

"Wow, what a great story! I also like your name, man. It sounds so heroic and awesome. Why didn't you try to use your real name in all the wrestling matches instead of Rhino? Your real name is 10 times better than an animal name, you know." Fartan said.

"The man in charge of all the games came to my forest. He accidentally passed many loud farts right in front of some women taking a bath in the river. He did not pay any close attention to his surroundings while farting his butt off. Then, one of the ladies was angry with me for farting over and punishing that big stinky animal in an almost cruel way. She forced him to use my nickname "Rhino" instead of Triden in all his official sporting paperwork. He told me he had to do it. Otherwise, that woman would have gone to our leader. She would have complained that he had seen her naked in the river. Our leader would have considered it as a big crime, you know. His severe punishment would have been excruciating tortures by the farts of all forest witches." He responded.

"So, that's how the great invincible Triden became Rhino in the eyes of all spectators. I guess that only happens to a man like you." Fartan laughed out loud.

Triden looked around the lunch table. He had no idea who the two beautiful women were sitting next to him. He asked Fartan to introduce everyone. The two beautiful young women looked at each other and smiled.

"This is Bella, my number one fan and the most beautiful woman of my life. We always enjoy farting together whenever we are alone. Bella is brilliant and very talented. She loves smelling my farts, and I love smelling hers, too. And the two hot ladies are Jordana and Lillian. The green-eyed blonde one sitting on your right side is Jordana, and of course, the blue-eyed brunette one on your left is Lillian. They are both Bella's close friends." He said.

"It's so wonderful to meet you all. Bella, thank you for being a good woman to Fartan! Jordana and Lillian, ladies, thank you for waking me up with the caressing of your lovely hands. Your charming beauty is breathtaking." He said.

"Make no mistake, my friend! If you think their beauty is their only best quality, just wait until they take away your breath by their magnificent art of farting. They both can control and change the smell of their farts any way they want. They can easily make it smell like a horse or a donkey's Fart or any other animal. They are both some of the most precious gassy treasures of Fartista. I am sure they can teach you so much about using your Fart any time you need it the most." He smirked.

"In that case, it's just a pure joy to have them around." Triden smiled.

Triden enjoyed the fact that most people liked the company of Fartan. Many people had watched him sharing his food with the poor and buying different gifts for children. Bella told him how Fartan was always helping out the less fortunate people who needed assistance in life.

"Fartan, forgive me, my friend! I was wrong about you. I thought you only won all the tournaments to be the army leader. I now see you were doing it just to help out your people. You are a true champion with a good heart. "God, I love being your friend. You are the best." Triden said.

"You have done nothing wrong. You are Lord Triden, the sole protector of the green forest. We both put up a big show back there in the ring right before the match. That is just for public entertainment.

It never means that any of us is a terrible person. But I like to learn to throw a punch like you. When you punched my chin, I felt like you almost chopped off my head." Fartan said.

"Oh, come on, man! You took away my eyesight in a matter of seconds without even hitting my eyes or even getting close to me. You didn't even touch any part of my body. What was that? That looked like a perfect move of skilled witchcraft disguised as a famous champion. How did you even do it? How did you use your power to knock me down so quickly from afar? I have never seen anything like it. There is still so much we both need to learn." He said.

"Ok, Triden! Why don't you stick around for a few more days? See if you enjoy our city, the company of Fartistans, our culture, and our customs! We can both share our fighting skills. I'll make it worth your while." Fartan said.

Triden invited Jordana and Lillian to have lunch with him on Friday afternoon. They were happy to accept his offer. He decided to stay for a few more days and check out the entire city of Fartista. Fartan paid the check plus the tips. They left the restaurant. Fartan asked Triden to accompany him to the army building the next day.

"Ok, Mr. Champion! Don't forget we are getting together for lunch this Friday! Bring Bella with you, too!" Triden said.

The following morning, Fartan went to the local inn to take Triden to the Army Center. It was a 15-minute walk from the inn.

They reached the center. The entrance guards stopped them and asked for their documents.

"I am Fartan. I won yesterday's Inter-City championship, and I am here to apply for the Army Leader position. This paper is my sealed winning letter. We are not carrying any sealed weapon such as small knives or a dagger at all. You can frisk and search both of us." He said.

"And who is this man, Fartan? Is he with you?" The guard asked.

"Oh, this is Lord Triden, the supreme protector of the green forest. He is a good friend of mine. I fully trust him." He said.

"You two, pull out your right hands. I must stamp you with a temporary pass seal. Remember, you can tour anywhere you want in the building. However, if a guard doesn't allow you to enter a specific area or a room. That means that area is off-limit. You must not go there. Is that understood?" The guard said.

"Yes, Sir. We will fully comply with all your rules. You have my word." Fartan said.

Triden and Fartan walked around the building and saw many young soldiers in military training. Triden was surprised when he saw a room full of well-crafted solid black cloth face masks in different sizes. He pointed his index finger towards them.

"Do your people use these on a battlefield? Why do you have them in your military?" He asked.

"Well, you are in Fartista. This land has the best farters in the entire globe. We are famous for using the power of our gross, stinky farts. I am not sure about the actual military application of these masks. But I guess when our soldiers fart on a battlefield, they wear their masks ahead of time to make sure they don't breathe their stinky farts and don't fall to the ground instead of the enemy forces. When all tactics fail, we start using the power of our foul gas. The army never attacks any other countries. Our land is one of the most resourceful lands in the world. Our soil comes bearing many precious natural gifts in it. If you ride your horse for a day or two, you will come across many different mines of precious metals such as gold, lead, and copper. We only practice self-defense to protect our people and our land. We also train our minds not to abuse the power of human biological gas for any evil purposes." He said.

A few days later, Lord Triden left Fartista to return to the green forest. He also invited Fartan and his beautiful sweetheart, Bella, to his home in the green forest.

A year passed. Fartan shared all his winning money with all the poor people. Fartan went on to finish all his challenging military training with the highest honors and awards. He became the most loved and mightiest army leader and commander in the entire land of Fartista. He told everyone that he would always be loyal to his King and family. He also trained all his soldiers how to use the secret power of their farts to return home victorious. Many tribes tried to attack Fartista and plunder all the resources and precious metals. They underestimated Fartan's leadership capabilities and fighting skills. He created the best-united army with all his loyal soldiers.

They won many wars without any bloodshed. Gradually, Fartan built one of the most potent farting armies the world had ever seen.

Soon, the old King Fartles made a grand public announcement. Unfortunately, the royal family died during an earthquake. He was the only one who was left alive. He was highly heartbroken, sad, and depressed. He had deeply cried and mourned the significant loss of all his loved ones for the past six long months.

King Fartles asked all people to gather around in the main entrance yard of his palace.

"Silence, the King of Fartista has arrived. All, hail the glorious King!" The royal announcer shouted.

Everyone knelt to the ground and bowed to the tremendously glorious King Fartles.

"Hear me out! As you know, six months ago, I lost my whole family in the earthquake. I hopelessly tried to save them. But, alas, I could not keep any of them alive. They died tragically right in front of my eyes. I lost my son "Jaden," my daughter "Jana," and my dear wife, "Lisa" altogether. There were many days that I almost wanted to die only to join my family in death." The King said.

He had tears of despair and significant loss in his kind eyes. His teardrops slowly fell to the ground. Then, he sat down on his royal chair. He cleaned and wiped away his tears. He soon noticed that all his people were looking at him with tearful eyes and wishful heavy hearts. There was a massive silence all among the crowd. Fartistans never had any lousy memory from any member of the royal family. The genuine kindness and love that the royal family showed to the people made the whole land the best place to live. They were famous for being the best rulers in all neighboring lands. Many foreigners traveled to Fartista only to stay and live there.

"Today, as your King, but more importantly as your leader, I, king Fartles, am standing in front of you to show my heartfelt gratitude. Thank you for mourning with me! It has been my most tremendous honor to be your King. It has been a joy to be the leader of Fartista for the past few decades. I am sorry if any of you, my good people, have gone through a difficult time because of me. I will never forget the happy days when my deceased son Jaden and Fartan ran around the city as two little kids. I always enjoyed watching them both growing up into strong good young men." The King said.

"Please, God! Grant me the necessary strength and a tougher spirit to go through life without my family!" He shed tears while he was speaking.

Once again, Fartistans had won the war against their enemies without any bloodshed. Thanks to their intelligent hero Fartan and his superior and effective gas-related strategies in different war zones. None of the families from enemies lost their men. Hence, they gladly and willingly agreed to join the victorious Fartistan empire. They now ruled one of the largest flatulence empires in the world.

"Today, I am rewarding Fartan, my other son, with the gift of the most respectable wedding ceremony in our land. The high commander Fartan and Bella are getting married. Let us honor, share and celebrate our victory through the true happiness of this wonderful, amazing young couple! I am hosting a big wedding party for Bella and Commander Fartan the day after tomorrow. Everyone is invited." The King said.

"Thank you, your majesty! I am truly speechless. You really are the greatest King who ever lived in our land." Fartan said.

"Fartan, my son!! Our nation and I acknowledge all your efforts and sacrifices. You are worthy of the best rewards. You lead with your Fart to defend our people. Your strength changes the outcome of any war for us. You also create and release the foulest farts on all battlefields. It is never easy to save this city using only your powerful farts, over and over again. Your wedding is your reward, my son. Go fetch your bride, now." The King said.

"Where is Bella? Find her! Please, don't tell her anything about the wedding yet!" Fartan asked his soldiers.

Fartan asked a few soldiers to decorate the yard with the most beautiful fresh red roses. They also brought an extremely vivid fascinating colorful dress for Bella.

Bella and the soldiers arrived. He looked at Bella and noticed she seemed surprised and shocked. She was worried about something.

"Oh, no! King Fartles and all his men must have known what I did yesterday. Did they finally find out I made a mess with my gas in the market yesterday? But who told them? I secretly relieved myself and let out a big one right next to the spice shop. More than 50 different scents were going out of that shop. How could they even spot and recognize my personal Fart out of all those various spice odors?" She thought. All those sinful and unrighteous thoughts attacked her mind instantly.

She looked around and saw the beautiful change in the palace yard. She knew then that no one had found out about her market incident at all.

"Oh, great! I am not here to get punished for yesterday." She whispered.

"Fartan, my love! What is going on? Have I done anything wrong?" Bella asked.

"No, my beautiful sweetheart! Of course, not! I just have a surprise for you. I wanted to ask you something important in front of the King and all the people." He answered.

"But first, you need to go and change into this beautiful dress. I bought it for you last night." He said.

"You did all of this just to make me happy? I love you so much." Bella said.

He stared at her tearful lovely, beautiful eyes. He always saw happiness in her face. Her eyes radiated true magnificent happiness and joy. The innocent, cheerful look in her eyes always brought back many delightful romantic memories for him. Who could ever forget about her glorious farting power?

However, it was much more than the farts that attracted him to her.

"I know. I love you too. Please, my darling! Go and change!"

He asked.

Fartan had given specific romantic instructions for the yard decoration methods. She grabbed the lovely dress and walked into the palace. All the flowers and the rose petals on the ground had a uniquely attractive setting. Furthermore, they brought the red royal chariot pulled by the two lovely white horses.

The royal maid applied and started the quick makeup rituals on Bella's face. Then she brought the dress for her.

"My lady, do you need any help changing into this dress?" she asked.

"No, I don't. Thank you! Call me, Bella! What's your name?" She asked.

"Jane!" She responded.

"Nice to meet you, Jane! Thank you for all your help today!" She said.

Bella changed into her new dress. Then, she let out a small fart just to make sure no gassy surprises were going out of her body in the yard in front of everyone. She walked towards the large mirror at the other side of the room.

It had a large window opening towards the backside of the palace. That was the room for all the palace ladies to change, apply makeup, get any necessary haircut, and perform hair coloring methods. The window provided a massive amount of essential light in the room.

Jane checked out Bella in her new dress. She enjoyed how beautiful and lovely she looked wearing the red dress. Bella looked into a mirror, turned around, and checked her backside, too.

"Wow, you look like an angel from heaven in this dress. He does know how to buy the most beautiful attire for you." She said.

"I do, don't I? Thank you, Jane!" She smiled.

"Ok, let's go! Everyone is waiting for us, outside." She said.

They walked towards the yard. As soon as they reached the door, the doorman shouted their arrival.

"Ladies and gentlemen, presenting Lady Bella!" He shouted.

She walked out the door into the palace yard. No one could take off their eyes from her. She looked extraordinarily breathtaking and beautiful in red.

The crowd cheered and yelled. "Long Live, Lady Bella: The Red Human Angel!"

Fartan was speechless. He was drooling all over the most beautiful, the sexiest, and the loveliest woman he had ever seen, his personal sweetheart.

"Wow, Bella! You look breathtaking. When I bought this outfit for you, I visualized how stunning you would look wearing it. Your heavenly beauty made my heart skip a beat. But I see now that you surpassed all my expectations as the most beautiful woman I have ever seen, my own lovely and beautiful sweetheart." Fartan said.

Then he knelt on his left leg, took out a small wooden box from his right pocket, opened it. He pulled it out in front of Bella. She lost the will and power to look away from that exquisite shining ring.

She saw one of the most beautiful weddings rings in the box. Fartan was proposing and asking for her hand in marriage.

"Lady Bella, you are my past, present, and my future all at the same time. I can never picture a day of my life without you. I even love how you use your fart power and how you enjoy farting with me simultaneously whenever we are alone together. Will you become my wife?" He asked.

"Yes, my darling! I will marry you in a heartbeat." Bella said.

Three days later, they got married. Bella looked far more beautiful than all other past brides in her white wedding dress.

"I vow to love you with all my heart, support you with all my kind spirit, hold you firmly in my arms when you feel sad. I also promise not to forget how the smell of your Fart made me madly fall in love with you. But above all, I make this vow to use my Fart only for the good of our society. I will be the best wind-breaking man as long as I live in this world." Fartan told Bella.

"Oh, my love! You are the only man who creates romantic wonders with his farts for me." She said.

"I love your creative farts, too. You're the only woman who can do so much with a single fart. If you want, you can use it to create a little gassy breeze or to confuse people around you, not knowing who did it in the first place." He said.

People were delighted and excited to be there at the wedding. Fartan and Bella performed many different styles of dances. Bella had the most relaxing and most delightful feelings both in her mind and her heart.

"Silence! Silence, everyone! King Fartles is making a new important announcement now."

The palace speaker yelled.

"One more thing, people! I am spending the last days of my life with you. The tragic loss of my loved ones took its painful toll on me. I would like to assign the next King and inform you who he is today. So, you may obey his orders and respect his kingdom on my behalf." King Fartles said.

"The next King will be commander Fartan. All hail Fartan, the new supreme ruler of Fartista!" The King said.

The entire crowd started cheering and got incredibly excited. All Fartistans knelt to the ground to display their respect for Fartan.

"No, my friends, my brothers, and sisters! Don't bow to me! Please, get up! I have always been only a man with far more responsibilities! Bow to your God who gave you the precious gift of life!

Bow to the beauty of your woman who gave you the gift of love and the divine gift of children! But above all, educate and train your children in our timeless traditional art of farting. Our ancient farting culture must never die with you. Every new generation inherits a gassy cultural gift from our forefathers. Always use the stinking power of your fart for good purposes. It must always get transcended from one generation to the next one." Fartan walked towards them and responded.

King Fartan and Bella lived their whole happy life together. They happily enjoyed smelling each other's farts for many decades. To keep the spark in their romantic marriage, they even invented creative farting fun activities together. The most exciting one was when they would stand apart a few yards from each other and bend over. Then they would both target the exact location of each other's anus and single-fire farts simultaneously. The two farts would impact each other, make a big kaboom sound, and then simply would neutralize each other in the air.

They continued that funny, gross activity even after they had their first child. Fartimus was their first-born son.

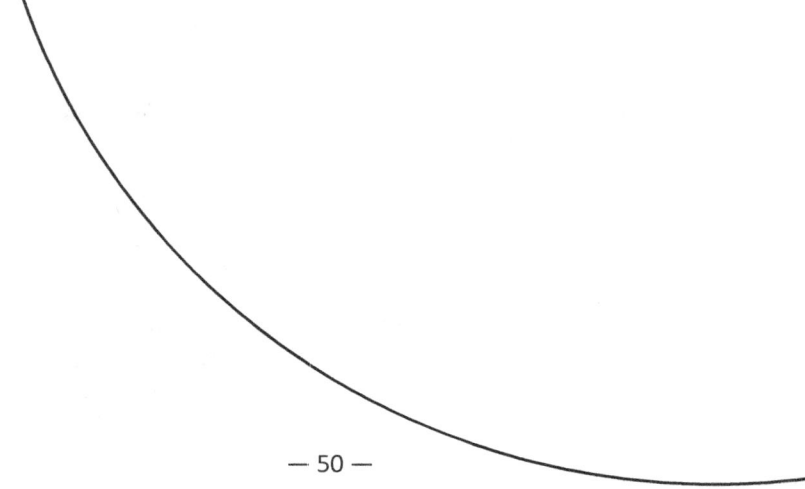

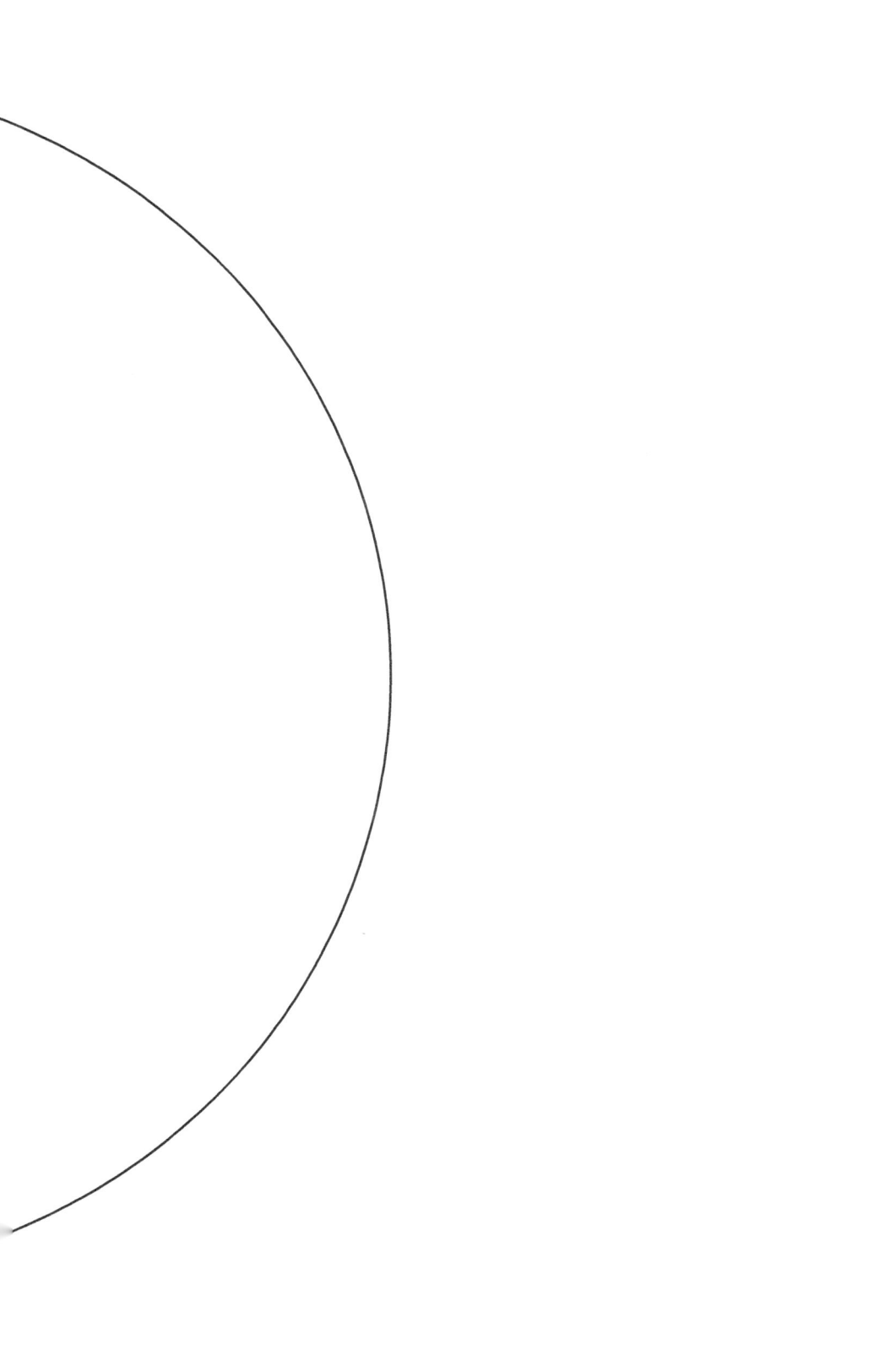

CHAPTER 4

The Elusive Farterella

This hilarious story takes place in the famous dreamy land of Fartista, where there was a royal flatulence party. King Fartan was getting aware that his gassy days were numbered. The royal family had a handsome young prince seeking a beautiful bride for his future coronation and throne. He was called Fartimus. You may recall that he was the King's oldest son. He was incredibly talented, intelligent, and skillful in the mysterious art of farting.

It was time to introduce Fartimus as the new King to the land. But there was a dire condition that needed quick attention from the royal family. After all, having a gassy bachelor prince as a future king was not pleasant for anyone. Therefore, they were looking for a beautiful, healthy young lady who could easily outnumber any other women just by using her powerful farts.

Then came the day of the event. Fartimus spotted a very sexy hot shapely young woman who displayed a mastery in the art of farting. Her farts were silent but deadly and crucially effective in destroying the fresh air all around it.

She was indeed the cunning witchcraft of all Farters in the world.

People called her: "The Elusive Farterella."

He approached her and politely invited her to attend the National Farting Championship contest. The winning prize was 5000 golden coins. It was enough to make anyone extremely rich and wealthy that they would never have to work again.

Fartimus slowly walked towards the beautiful young woman.

"Hi, there! I'm Prince Fartimus. What's your name?" He said.

"Hi, Fartimus! I'm Farterella. Nice to meet you!" She smiled and said.

"Hang on a second; you mean you're the one who raised the best and gassiest storms in the northern areas of my reign?" He asked.

"Yes, I am her." She said.

After they exchanged a few quick flirtatious sentences back and forth, he asked her how she became the mightiest Farter of the land.

She explained that during her childhood times, at bedtime, there was a fascinating lullaby story her late father was reading to her.

She used that old guru as her one and only malodorous role model to increase her self-development and farting powers.

The bedtime story goes as below:

Years ago, there was a Royal Flatulence Guru who was living in the palace. He could recognize and treat people's different sicknesses just by smelling their farts. He had a unique power to digest any food and turn it into the most disgusting, silent dry farts. You know the ones you notice long after their creators are gone.

People believed any time he was releasing gas. He could quickly make the nearest canary faint.

Farterella's father told her that he knew it was her destiny to accomplish great things in life by using her malodorous skills. She would have the same strength and invincible power to faint a canary from afar.

They decided to start the contest. There were a few caged canaries 200 inches above the ground. There was one separate cage set explicitly for each contestant in each line. Farters lined up. Per contest's regulations and rules, they stood up 500 yards away from each other in parallel lines. That rule was there to ensure the rivals could not cheat and take credit for other's farts in making the birds faint.

All contestants would wait for their assigned gas releasing time. There were also separate **CSA's** (Chief Smelling Agent) given to each malodorous contestant individually.

The King started the countdown from number four down to one. Soon, the farters began getting ready for the ultimate most fetid challenge of their life. In 15-minutes intervals, Farters started to release gas as hard as they could, one by one. Producing the most putrid and smelliest rapid Fart was the only way to win over the others.

Although, all contestants created the most disgusting gas ever to smell by any nose. However, they were not strong enough to use their orifice to target the canaries in the cages and make them faint from afar.

That gave Farterella a very significant winning opportunity. Since she was a female contestant, she was the last one to try her luck at winning. Then to everyone's immense surprise, as soon as she started her first Fart, her caged bird, along with three other canaries sitting and singing from the top of the nearby trees, got unconscious and fell from the trees instantly. It was a good boost for her confidence.

Per Fartimus' instructions, they had placed a pile of soft fabrics right below the trees and around them. As a result, none of the innocent birds got hurt when they fell from the trees.

Then, her smelling agent saw how she made the canaries temporarily faint from 100 yards away with a single fart. He quickly ran towards the King.

"Your majesty, please, stop the game, now. I have come to present the only winner for you. The winner is a woman." He said.

"Are you sure it was her?" The King asked.

"Yes, your majesty, it really was her. You see, as a CSA, I keep training my nose and smell the nastiest farts daily. Hence, I surely know how different a woman's fart smells." He said.

"There is gassy wisdom in your intelligent speech. Very well! I mean, why not? I am sure any woman can be as good as any man in anything. Where is she?" King Fartan said.

He pointed towards Farterella. Some of the male opponents were angry to lose their chance of a lifetime to a woman.

There was chaos bound to happen quickly among the crowd. Then a woman yelled: "Shut up and let the agent talk! This year only a woman is the best winner."

The crowd started to scream with happiness and excitement. The entire land had never seen a woman winning any tough contest. All the men realized that a farting woman could also be as good as any other farting man. They were too shocked by the final results.

"Silence, we have a lady winner. I give you the great Farterella. I truly enjoyed her great victory. It surely counts as the first, greatest, and most malodorous victory for all women. From now on, I'll allow any woman to attend any contest right along with other men. Farterella, please, move forward and be ready to receive your award." King said.

"Bring me the golden Farting award, which is 5000 golden coins." The King said.

The Chief Smelling Agent went to fetch the award for the King.

Farterella started to walk towards the King. Suddenly, the dark rainy clouds covered the whole blue sky. The heavy rain began to pour down. The palace was struck by the powerful lighting many times over and over again. One of the tree branches hit Fartimus' head, and he fell to the ground unconsciously. Moments later, the wind blew away the clouds. Fartimus felt dizzy and disoriented. He slowly opened his eyes and got up from the field. He saw many injured people there. The palace building and the enormous playground received considerable damage.

He looked for Farterella as far as his eyes could reach. Alas, she was out of his sight. The soldiers could not find her either. He was genuinely heartbroken. He sighed and had tears of regret in his eyes. For he had lost his only chance at having and keeping true love in his life.

"No, this can't be the end of our love. Where are you, my sweet, beautiful love? Farterella, I know you're alive somewhere. I'll find you, my love." He said.

If only Fartimus could find an efficient way to locate and recognize Farterella accurately among all other young women in town. He had to come up with an idea.

"What if I catch a canary and cage it, then knock at every door and ask their young women to fart towards the cage? That way, if the canary faints right away, I'll know for sure that I have found my lovely woman." He told himself.

Our brooding Fartimus assumed that finding his smelly sweetheart and a future queen for his throne would be easy-peasy. But as it turned out, spending days and days of long malodorous tedious hours of cage-to-butthole research was not an easy task. He was frustrated.

He left with his soldiers along with some of the palace's female servants. They all started walking around the town. They went door to door and searched all the homes one by one. Suddenly he saw two young women who somehow reminded him of Farterella. He felt they were Farterella's stepsisters. They had many evil thoughts in their minds. They came up with a new scheme. What if all women in town would not wipe their buttholes after using the bathroom? That way, Fartimus' nose would indeed never work after smelling so much crap. Thus, he could never find Farterella. They could both seduce him with their farts. He thought they were crazy enough to expect him not to notice their apparent malodorous deception. Alas, he had no idea that they had sent his sweetheart to a distant village away from the city.

"What else can I do but to find her? Give up on my love for a heavenly sexy hot woman who loves my Fart as much as I love hers? No way! Nothing can stop me from finding her. That's a promise. I'll keep her sweet love in my heart until the day I find her." He told himself.

The young, handsome prince began his long royal quest for his smelly young bride. He and his female servants went door to door. He knew she lived somewhere in town.

He ordered them to perform concrete smelling ritual steps to recognize and find her. They needed to let any young woman lift her skirt, turn around, bend over, and release gas toward the canary cage.

Meanwhile, he was watching the whole process in every townhome. There was no exception for the smelling ritual. He ordered that all young ladies present in any home, including the maidens, attend the quest ceremonies.

They tried the dainty cage on the butthole of every eligible young maiden in the land. It was exhausting, extraordinarily malodorous, and grueling work. Thus, they had to take many breaks to get fresh air every ten minutes. They knew there was no other way to find Farterella. Their faces changed color and turned white so many times.

Remember that the origins of this story go back to medieval days. It was way before the invention of Charmin Ultra Soft toilet tissues. The prince and his ladies' team often came across young maidens who had not removed their poop from their buttholes entirely before participating in the search rituals. They had to inhale the smell of farts, which were as gross as piles of the manor. The results were disastrous during those smelliest moments.

There was no other way. Time was of the most critical essence. They knew that soon they would be rewarded with inhaling the best, driest, and most fantastic type of Fart in their time, Farterella's Fart.

But eventually, Fartimus' extended tedious foray into flatulence paid off. He found the woman who had captured his heart forever.

Then on the seventh day of their quest, while he was riding the new royal, red-colored coach through the rural roads. Fartimus and his team came across a large village.

They saw a sign right above the main village entrance door.

It read:

"Welcome, to Malodora Village! Be conservative with your farts! Always, Be Cautious, where and when you fart your ass off!"

He ordered the Malodorian village elders to gather around all young ladies. Then, they placed the canary cage on a stage at least 200 inches above the ground.

Suppose they could find a woman who could make the canary faint from 100 yards away with a single fart. Then they knew they had found their ideal candidate.

Meanwhile, men could only watch the whole thing in dreadful silence. No man could make any embarrassing comments or gestures towards the young ladies who were attending the event.

He knew she was there. Then they started the event. Young ladies lined up. They approached the stage one by one. They turned around while their butt pointed the scene of the caged bird, lifted their skirts, bent over, targeted the cage with their buttholes, and released their strongest farts ever.

The competition was fierce. Many contestants tried, did their best, and failed miserably. After all, every young woman wanted to be the future queen. So, you can easily imagine how they went the extra mile and worked their asses off to win the prince's heart.

Then came a time when a straightforward young woman tried her luck at winning. She moved towards the front stage, stood behind the line, turned around, lifted her old weary skirt, bent over, and farted without trying as hard as others.

Seconds later, everyone was shocked to see how the canary fainted so easily. The crowd got so excited and hoorayed the beautiful young winner.

Fartimus jumped down from his chair, ran towards her without any hesitation.

"Farterella, my love. I have finally found you." He yelled. He hugged her, held her beautiful face in his hands, stared into her magical eyes, and kissed her sexy pouty lips passionately.

"I too love you and your farts so much, Fartimus." She said.

They went on stage. Fartimus held her in his arms, pulled aside his chair, and asked her to sit down.

"Malodorians, listen up. Today, I am having the happiest day of my life. I finally found the woman of my dreams after smelling so many malodorous farts. I have been smelling the farts from hell. It was as if all those other women simply sat on my face and just farted all over my face. My nose cannot function for the time being. But I will be fine in a matter of a day or two. I have deprived myself of the gift of smell so that I could find my love. Today is the day that I have found her. I would love to show my appreciation to you all. Starting today, as your King, but most importantly, as your friend, I Fartimus, the New King of Fartista, will give you many privileges over the others. Together, we will create and build our dreamland, a land that justifies and displays the real power of farts in the entire world. Now, let us enjoy our time and have a great wedding party here later!" He said.

Days later, King Fartan and his Royal family arrived at the Malodora Village. They decorated the whole village with the most beautiful ornaments, flowers. Fartimus purchased new clothes for the entire villagers. He made sure that everyone was happy and well-fed. People were joyful about his extraordinary kindness.

Fartan was the only and the best malodorous prince who also owned a kind heart.

He always wanted a desirable life partner for all his exciting malodorous adventures. A woman who enjoyed passing gas as much as he did. A female partner who knew the proper places and rules for releasing gas like him.

They got married, enjoyed smelling each other's farts for many years to come.

Fartimus learned to focus on more political ways of passing gas in public, like practicing his public display of flatulence. He discovered that if he had to break the wind and it was during his speech for people. He could do it next to the nearest large animals such as horses, donkeys, and mules. Then he could easily blame them for the act of farting.

He even scheduled more quality times to fart together with Farterella more often.

And thanks to Farterella's precision Farting targeting system, any time they wanted to take a short daytime nap together. She could temporarily silence all the singing canaries with her Fart.

Years passed. Our happy royal married couple took advantage of their unique love and ability to move gas to publish their new book. They created and released the first book of Passing Gas at Proper Places throughout the land.

Fundamentally, the first book trained all future generations on the basic proper etiquette of farting and ways to avoid public and personal embarrassment. You see the practical results from the complex and lengthy lifetime joint work of Fartimus and Farterella together in today's societies.

Unfortunately, that book vanished through the dust of time. But science proves that there are solid Fartimus and Farterella genes in all of us.

They lived a long smelly, gross marital life and sat over each other's faces and released gas happily ever after.

CHAPTER 5

Introducing the All-New Fart Clinic

The Fart Clinic

From the dawn of medical science, humans have been searching for a way to cure and comfort patients struggling with severe gassy issues.

Never before no one thought about the idea of a clinic explicitly built for the sole purpose of flatulence treatments. Fortunately, the famous Dr. B. A (Big Ass) Fartin, also suffering from this awful disease, created a Fart Clinic.

At the age of eight, he got infected with CFS (**C**ontinuous **F**latulence **S**yndrome). He stunk his entire childhood neighborhood surroundings many times.

Later, he pursued medical school to become a doctor and help any patient suffering from painful diseases one day.

Years later, he opened up the clinic under honorable medical intentions. He placed an exciting ad in all medical journals informing patients about this flatulence clinic's crucial existence.

The ad went as the following:

The Fart Clinic

Hurry and Visit Us!

We have improved our latest services for all different types of farting patients.

We offer a speedy, quick, affordable, timely cure and effective treatment turnaround for all your gross gas-related issues.

You can never blame yourself if you have turned into the fart machine. See our doctor and finally get cured.

We currently accept all major insurance plans and monthly payment plans. In return, we only ask that you seriously avoid eating the rotten tomatoes and eggs, dead cow's meat, and all other smelly foods for your breakfast or lunch right before visiting us.

Let us be completely honest with you! Who in our clinic knows how terrible, how gross, and how disgusting your Fart is?

Recently, we have been approved for a large loan from our bank. As a result, we equipped all our waiting rooms with some of the most advanced fully automatic ventilation systems.

Overall, our priority is to help you stay alive. We will take care of all your gassy needs in our clinic. We guaranty your safety while you are sitting down in our waiting rooms. It merely removes the terrible danger of your instant suffocation.

Your doctor will thoroughly check and examine your digestive systems and your butthole to evaluate the effects of your farts on others.

A Biography about Your Doctor

Dr. B. A (Big Ass) Fartin has been practicing professionally since

1991. He is originally from Fartista. However, he grew up in America in many different states. His father was a traveling Car Insurance salesman. They lived and traveled thru many various States. As a result, Dr. Fartin received first-hand social experience of being with so many different people from all walks of life.

He is an established and highly skilled doctor with over thirty years of experience. He is well regarded worldwide in the field of Human gas release issues.

His passion is driven by the professional bonds he creates with his patients throughout their ongoing farts analysis and continuous treatments. He loves seeing patients recover so they can use their farts like all other healthy people, again.

He is highly recommended by the WFO (**W**orld **F**latulence **O**rganization). In 1988, he graduated at the top of his class. During his internship, he decided to change medical history forever.

His massive research medical skills have astounded the world of science over and over again. The medical world will never forget the sacrifices that he endured during his life-threatening research.

He traveled worldwide to perform many actual long and tedious flatulence tests both on humans and animals. He courageously volunteered to smell many human and animal butts while passing gases.

Once, an elephant and a big baboon accidentally released a large amount of gross gas all over his face simultaneously. The poor doctor was unconscious for days after that terrible incident. He lost his power of smell for a few weeks altogether.

He went into a coma having terrifying nightmares. Later, he mentioned that he was getting tortured by the big angry animals with the enormous butts in the jungle.

He explained what chilling hallucinations were showing. In them, he was always tied up to the ground. Then, the large animals were lining up to Fart all over his face one by one. We are glad he survived through all those gross experiments and restless research.

Today, Dr. Fartin has held many seminars, written books, and short pamphlets on controlling your butt properly while attending different gatherings, what to eat, daily toilet schedule, etc.

He is the international official medical representative of the WFO.

In addition to his gassy practice, he is also the head of the AFAP (**A**merican **F**resh **A**ir **P**reservation) academy. He takes great pride in the special care and effective treatment of all patients who have had to deal with their gas problems.

In your first appointment, he explains the benefits of daily butt exercise, safety precautions (such as releasing your gross gas only in toilets, mountains, and forests rather than doing it in all closed environments.) You will also learn how to save money by purchasing the best ventilation system for your home.

Rest assured; you are in good hands. For all your fart-related questions and concerns, talk to Dr. Fartin. Your doctor will answer all your questions.

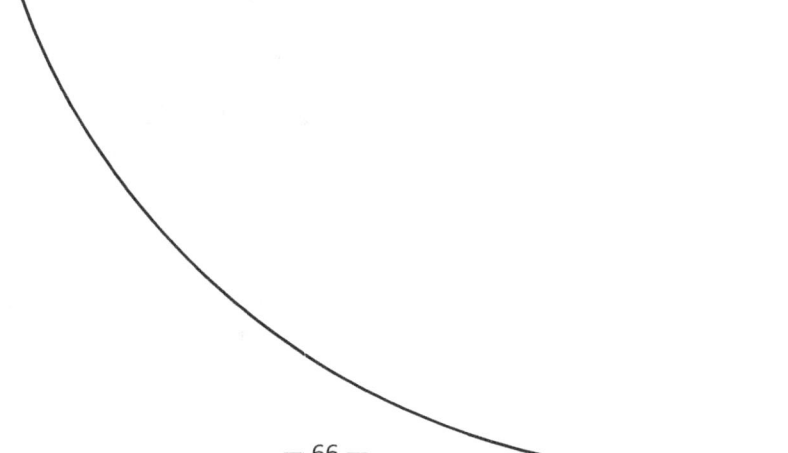

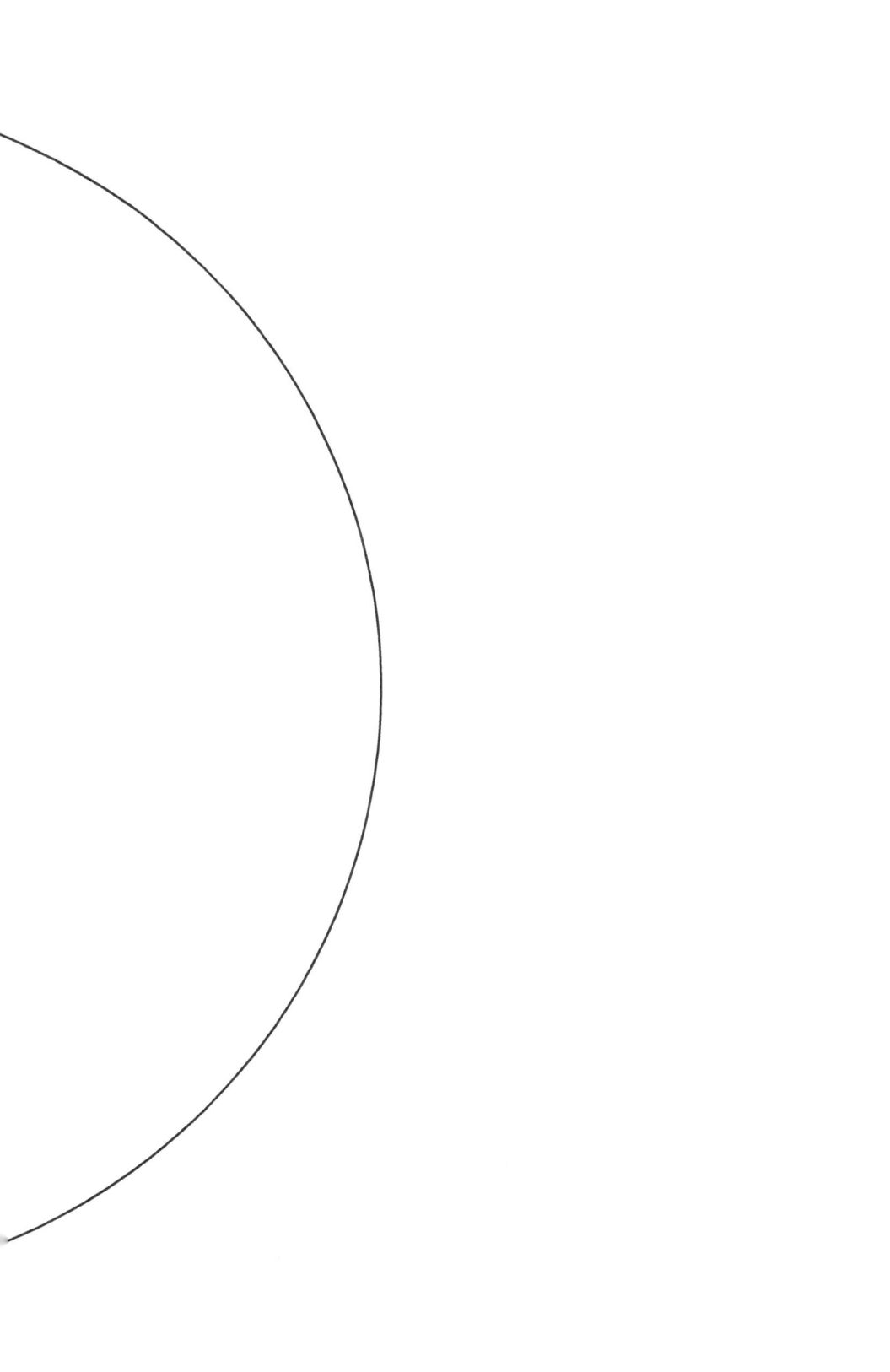

CHAPTER 6

The Untold Ancient Truth Behind Jacuzzi

Once a king wanted to create the best entertainment and most generous public feasts for all the people in ancient Persia.

He thought if people liked his dinners and enjoyed them. He would get elected as the great King once again.

King Darius, the Great Ruler, was a kind man who enjoyed seeing his entire country happy.

On top of his appropriate administrative methods and grand building projects, he also displayed unconditional kindness towards different people under his rule.

One of his most prominent characteristics was how he never took himself seriously in all public parties and celebrations.

One of his most favorite hobbies was about how people hysterically laughed at someone who was freely and carelessly farting around even in the presence of the great King.

Then came a time for the New Year celebration, which was precisely at the beginning of Spring.

While very drunk, he was the first to call the Persian language "Fartsi" instead of "Farsi." The instant hilarious reaction of all attendants was highly satisfying. Some of them pissed their pants and even farted their asses off out of sheer laughter.

Then, he decided to invite his close friend Sheikh Goozoo. He was indeed one of the first Persian forerunners in the complex ancient art of farting.

He could easily fart all over the party, and nobody would even notice it until it was already too late for taking any action against him.

The Persians were one of the first nations who created two different words for their farts.

Suppose the Persians would release their gas with a loud noise. They would call it Gooz.

However, if the Fart was going out of their body without any noticeable sound. Then, they would call it "Choss."

Suppose you know anyone who farts masterfully and never gets caught in any public place. You need to know about the fact they have mastered changing their big farts (Gooz) into a Choss (a small unnoticeable silent fart).

After all, if you can never hear it happening. How are you going to catch the responsible one? By the time you smell the gross air, the sneaky and crafty Farter is long gone.

Back to our story, Darius asked Sheikh Goozoo to develop the hilarious idea to make the royal party much more pleasant for everyone.

Soon, Sheikh Goozoo made an official announcement about a Royal Flatulence Competition. Everyone was welcome to take part in the competition.

There was only one official rule. Whoever could create the best and most effective Fart will be the winner of 5000 golden coins.

All challengers signed a leather non-disclosure affidavit stating that they would never use their farts for any evil purposes against the

Royal family, the current government, and all the people.

Then, all participants lined up. They painted a big circle on the floor away from the party. It was right below a vent on the ceiling. The vent had the power to suck the gross air out very effectively.

The winner was the one who could make a hole right in the center of the Fart circle.

Darius started the countdown from ten to zero for the game to begin. As soon as he got to zero, the first contestant left the line, entered the Fart Circle, sat down, removed his pants, and released his loudest Fart as hard as possible. People started laughing hysterically right after they heard the loud bang coming out of the first man.

The same act got repeated by all female and male competitors, too.

However, no one was able to create a hole in the floor. The players were all tired and restless out of releasing their gas most powerfully.

Finally, the King called Sheikh Goozoo and said: "Well, my dear friend, it seems to me that this is a job that only you can handle. Now, go and show us all how you would have done it, in the first place."

Sheikh Goozoo stood up and walked towards the circle. He removed his pants, sat down, placed both his wide-opened legs right in the middle of the ring. Then he whispered a chant and looked up, positioned both of his palms together, and let out the most massive fart of his entire wind-breaking career.

The mighty Fart was so powerful that it created a huge hole right below where he was sitting. He fell right inside on lots of lukewarm water and started making many happy noises out of having sheer fun of just being in that lukewarm freshwater.

Later, the King summoned his best architects and brick-layers crew to create a remarkable bathtub out of that hole. He called it: "JaaGoozi" (Jaa: the place of, Goozi: Fart).

They simply used this bathtub for farting under the water. That was the very first miniature swimming pool used solely for releasing gas under the water. It was extremely relaxing, convenient, and hilarious to go inside it and enjoy submerging in it.

They created a tub-shaped area big enough for six to seven people. All the interior bottom and walls were made with attractive colorful marbles. One intelligent architect came up with a unique design for using bamboo trees as pipes to direct the flow of warm water to the holes all around the bottom of the interior walls.

To avoid slipping, everyone was wearing swimming sandals while submerging in the JaaGoozi. There were also cloth face masks ready and available right next to it. They used them to stay alive while farting their butts off in the JaaGoozi.

Almost three thousand years later, the renowned English Sir "Fart-A-Lot" secretly traveled to Iran, stole that entire idea, and took it to Britain. He changed the name to Jacuzzi. Then he received the highest rewards and recognition from Queen Elizabeth. She called him the man with a fascinating creative mind.

He took all newfound credit for creating and inventing a Jacuzzi.

What you see in today's world as a Jacuzzi initially came from the ancient land of Persia.

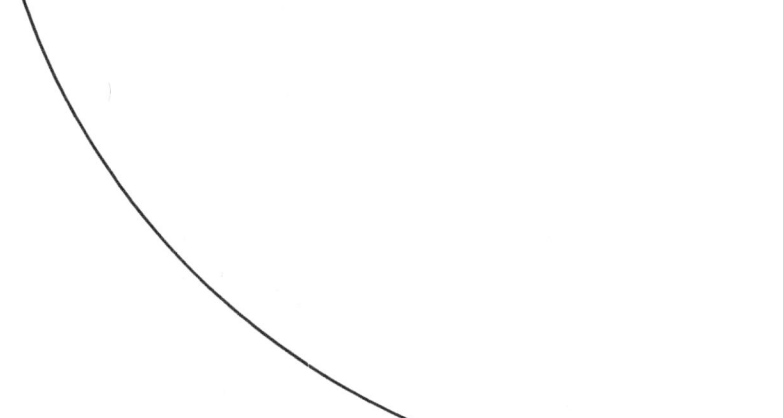

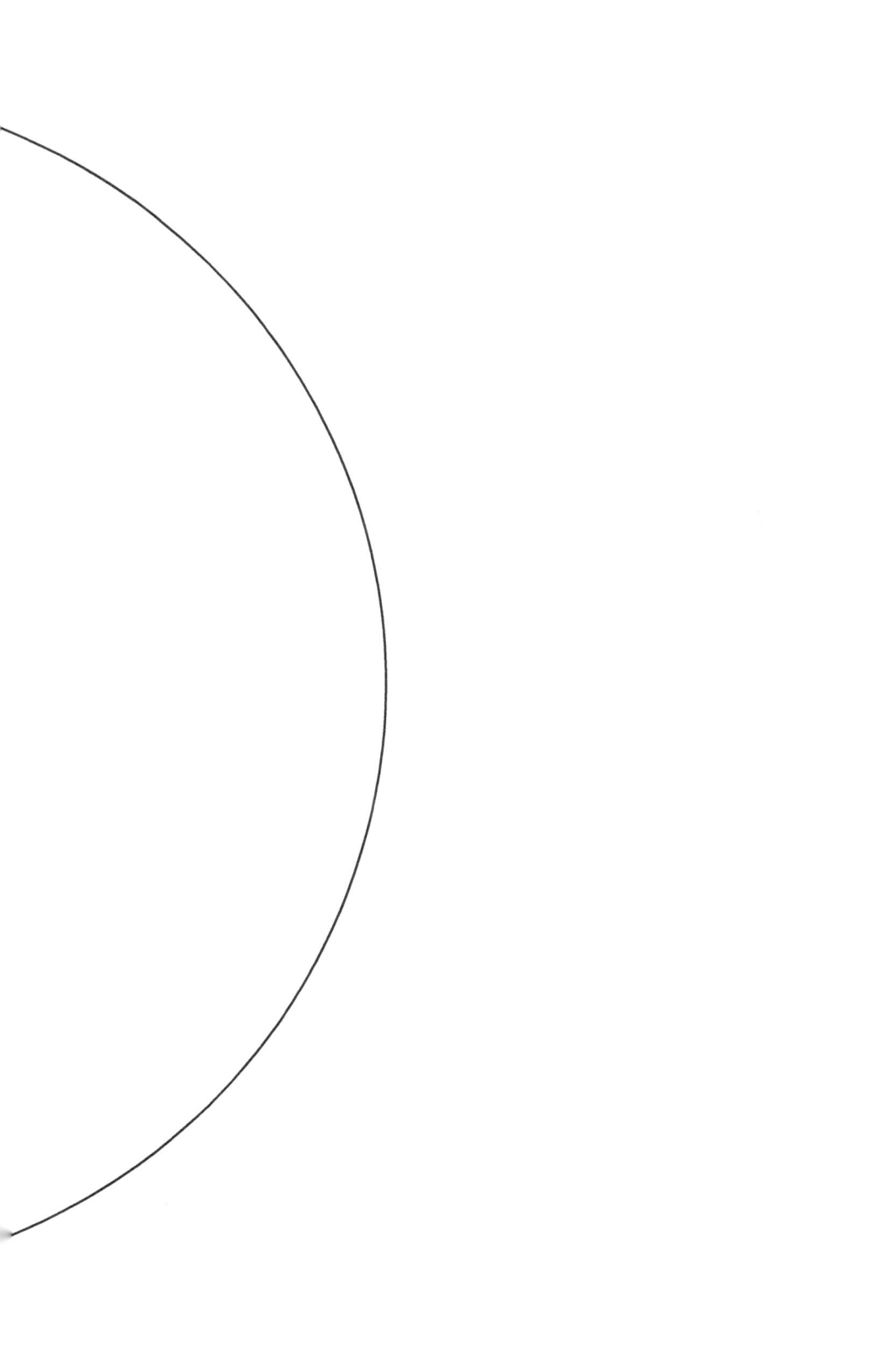

CHAPTER 7

The Lifesaving Farting Lessons

(The Ultimate Survival Guide for All Farters)

If you have ever secretly thought about farting and creative ways to blame others for doing it. Then you have the potential to be misguided and follow the dark side of your soul to ruin the fresh air for all the good-doers. Those are the ones who tried their best to hold it in until they had found and emptied themselves in a bathroom.

Therefore, in a sense, you did not have to release a massive loud gross fart to be considered a farter in the first place.

That undeniable fact about you never makes you a terrible person at all. Why is that? Because we all have dark sides when it comes to doing good versus evil. I have thought about it, too.

While releasing gas any time you feel pressured by your body and evil side seems a straightforward and most convenient solution for getting rid of a gassy problem. You must remember to follow the goodness of your soul and do the right thing all the time.

The right thing is to let your butt go crazy with farting only in a bathroom or while you are hiking in the mountains, forests, wild parks only when you are sure you are entirely far away from others. That ensures no other humans, or any animals have to suffer the consequences of your silly gassy gross decisions in any way.

Always remember to be thoughtful and considerate about animals too! If you release a giant gas and it lands right over an animal's face, unintentionally.

You are in big trouble. If the animal happens to be a flesh-eating animal such as big cats, wolves, coyotes, or hyenas. Then you are facing an imminent danger of seriously getting hurt by them.

Imagine what would happen if you farted over the face of the male lion. The King of the Jungle would never go easy on you. You better be driving your car while doing it. Otherwise, that pissed-off sultan of the forest will try his best to catch you and hurt you for good.

On the other hand, you simply have no idea about how gross and how awful your Fart is at the moment of hitting an animal's face. That moment has the potential to turn even the calmest and most peaceful animals, such as the little birds, into a raging angry foe against you.

You now have to deal, run, and stay away from the furious little animals that looked such lovely creatures moments ago, right before you farted all over their faces.

Suppose you have a hard time grasping that simple concept. Then I will tell you a truly shocking story about my childhood times.

Years ago, I had finished and graduated the last year of primary school with the highest grades. Then my late father took the whole family to visit my grandparents while they were working. I was on top of the world.

Both my grandfathers were skilled and hardworking farmers. They had been working in their agriculture careers their whole lives. They had a small cottage made entirely out of clay and haystack. It was large enough to hold a few people in it. It also had a small wooden solid door.

We went to their farms. My paternal grandfather also had many different fruit trees, such as black figs, apples, apricots, cherries, and grapes.

My favorite ones were always the fig trees. As a result, I picked a reasonably tall fig tree, climbed it, and started eating the tasty, juicy, delicious black figs one by one.

There was only one thing on my mind. I wanted to eat the black figs as much as possible. While I was eating impatiently, suddenly, I felt the need to fart and relieve myself. Hence, I released a very loud and my most gross Fart ever. I ultimately failed to notice the tiny nest of sparrows right below my butt.

Then, I felt a sharp pain right over my back. I noticed that an angry male sparrow had hit and attacked me. You see, my big smelly Fart had rendered the tiny birds in the nest almost lifeless.

I chose to fight off the small angry father rather than run away and forget to eat the figs. I hit it with the palm of my right hand slowly. It fell on the ground without getting injured in any way. He rose and let a big scream out of his beak.

Soon, I saw a small cloud of sparrows coming towards me. My father yelled: "Get down now and run for your life! Just go hide somewhere, quickly!"

So, I quickly climbed down the tree and ran straight towards the cabin. I quickly got inside, covered up the small window, and locked myself inside the cottage.

The angry sparrows started hitting the wooden door with their tiny beaks. It was one of the scariest experiences I have gone through in my entire life.

They used their tiny beaks of fury to teach me a valuable lesson. The hitting sound of tens of hundreds of small and ferocious beaks was getting louder and louder. Who would have thought a single malodorous fart would create a matter of life and death for me?

It went on for almost one hour. Then, as luck would have it, my paternal grandfather had two extremely lazy donkeys who were only famous for eating grass, being extremely lazy, and releasing the grossest gas. I even knew many sneaky farters who always blamed those two four-legged animals for getting out of many horrendous situations.

He came to my rescue. He had both donkeys standing side by side while they had their big asses aiming at the heart of the cloud of angry birds.

He slapped their big bellies one by one by the palm of his right hand. That created a chain fart reaction in both donkeys. They started releasing gas together as many times as possible. Soon, the little angry birds began falling from the sky, and many were unconscious for a short while.

They were no match for the potent gas of the sluggish donkeys. Almost twenty minutes later, they left the scene and never came back. Luckily none of them were injured in any way. I had peace of mind to know they would never try to get revenge on me later.

I promised myself not to fart and release gas in the presence of any big or small animal ever again.

Let that be a life-saving lesson to you all!

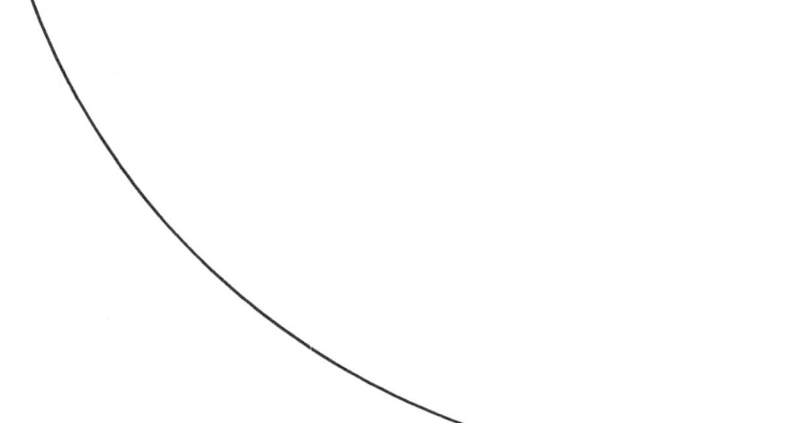

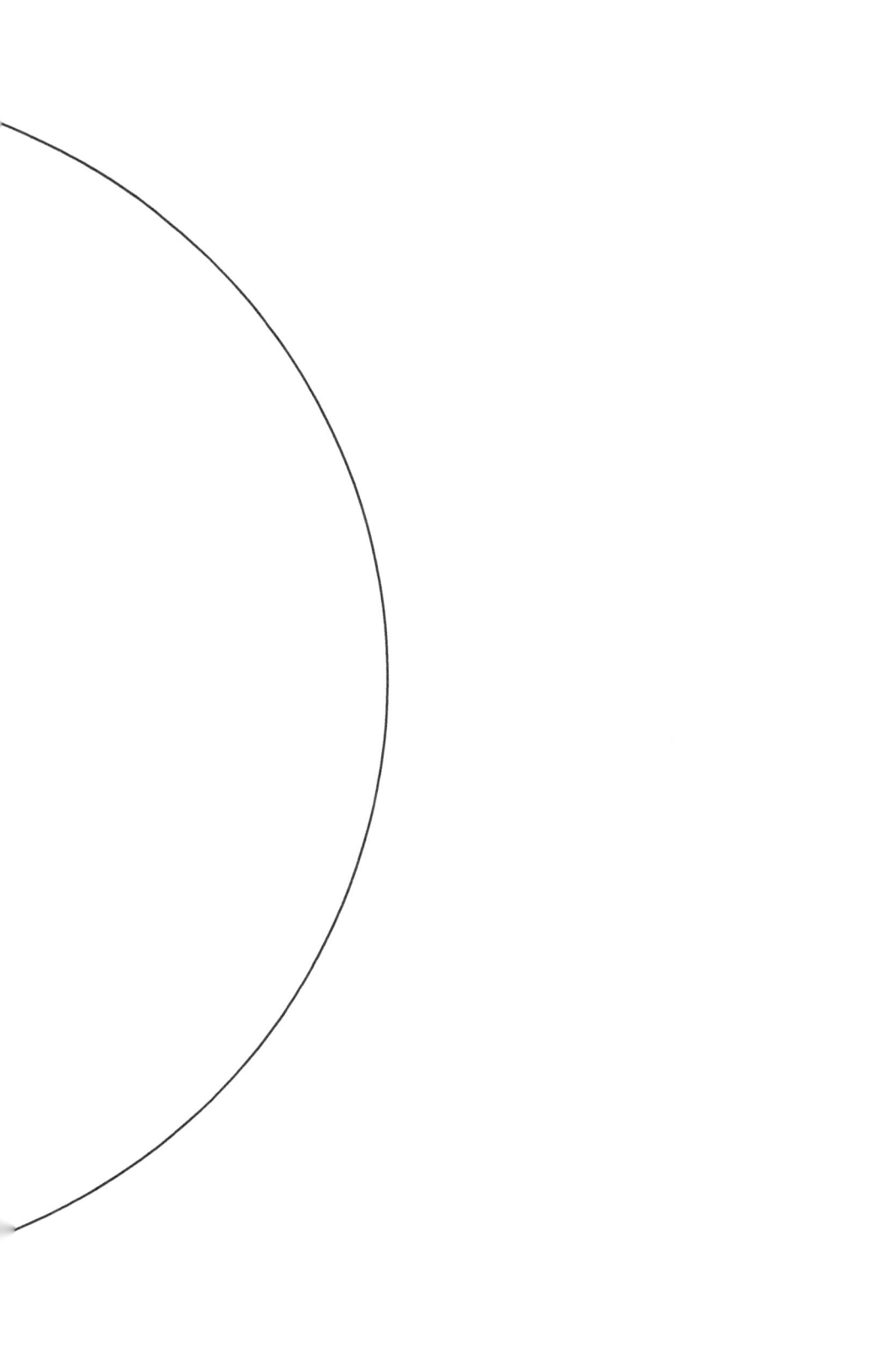

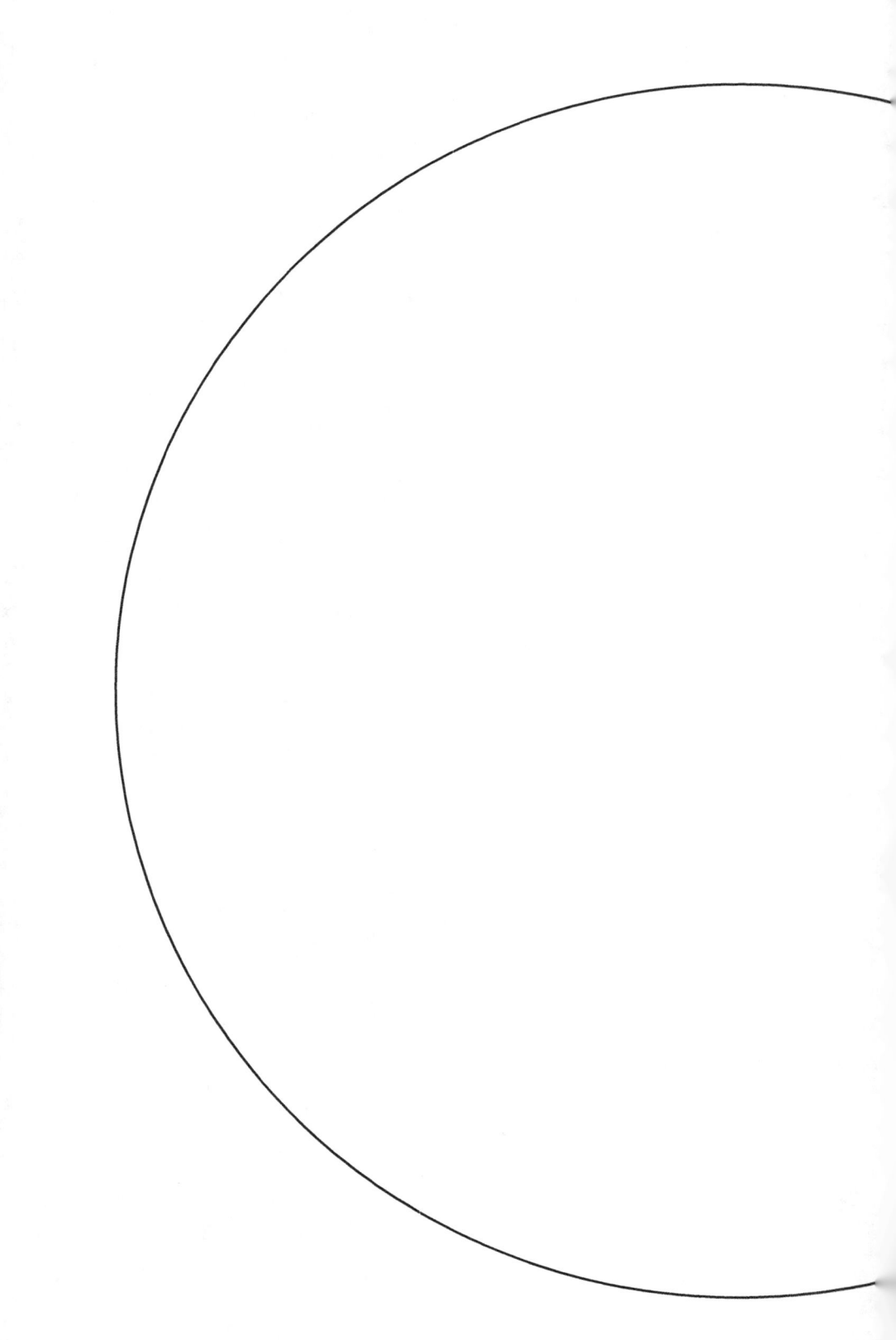

CHAPTER 8

Why Your Body Produces a Fart

Since the dawn of time, almost all humans have been baffled by the below question.

Why do we fart? But more importantly, why do we always get the severe burning urge to release gas at the most inappropriate places and times?

During eating your food, your digestive system creates a stockpile of foods that produces excessive gas. At the same time, while you are eating your food, you are also swallowing air.

When excessive gas and swallowed air get combined and accumulated in your body, that is precisely when your brain sends powerful signals to your digestive system.

Then your intestines get stimulated to move down your Fart to your rectum. The rectum is a tube passage leading to your anus. That is the only way for your body to get rid of the Fart as soon as possible.

There are times in life that you felt going to the bathroom to let your butt go wild, passing the most disgusting humanly made gases.

But then it was as if your intestines and your entire digestive system had failed you right at that exact moment.

So, what on earth was wrong with you? Were there out of this world forces compelling your body and mind faking your actual need to use the toilet?

I will tell you exactly what was wrong. It was never your fault at all. Your body has always trained your brain to use any excuses to view passing gas as the most relaxing and comforting bodily function ever. That is why you see people laugh hysterically when they hear the squeaky sound of a fart or when they grossly smell a silent one.

They all pretend to show resentment and disgust, but deep down, they all want to laugh their butt off instantly.

Think about it this way! When you are using the toilet seat, going about your business, whether small or the big one, wouldn't you always feel delighted and much better than the times your farts try their best to get out of your body any way possible?

How to Control the Act of Farting

Now that you have learned the logic behind creating your most embarrassing moments unintentionally. Perhaps, you can finally train your mind to control your bottom to push back that naughty small gas into your upper body until you get a chance to find the nearest toilet.

As the most important rule of thumb, always stop thinking of and laughing at any wind-breaking situation in any place! Once you start considering them as the most repulsive actions.

Gradually, you develop a normal tendency to despise any fart. When that occurs in your mind, your brain takes lasting mental notes of your disgust.

By then, your brain awareness increases into higher levels of understanding and learning about the destructive effects of releasing smelly gas anywhere it is happening. You are now well aware that you have built a new Fart-Free dimension in your life.

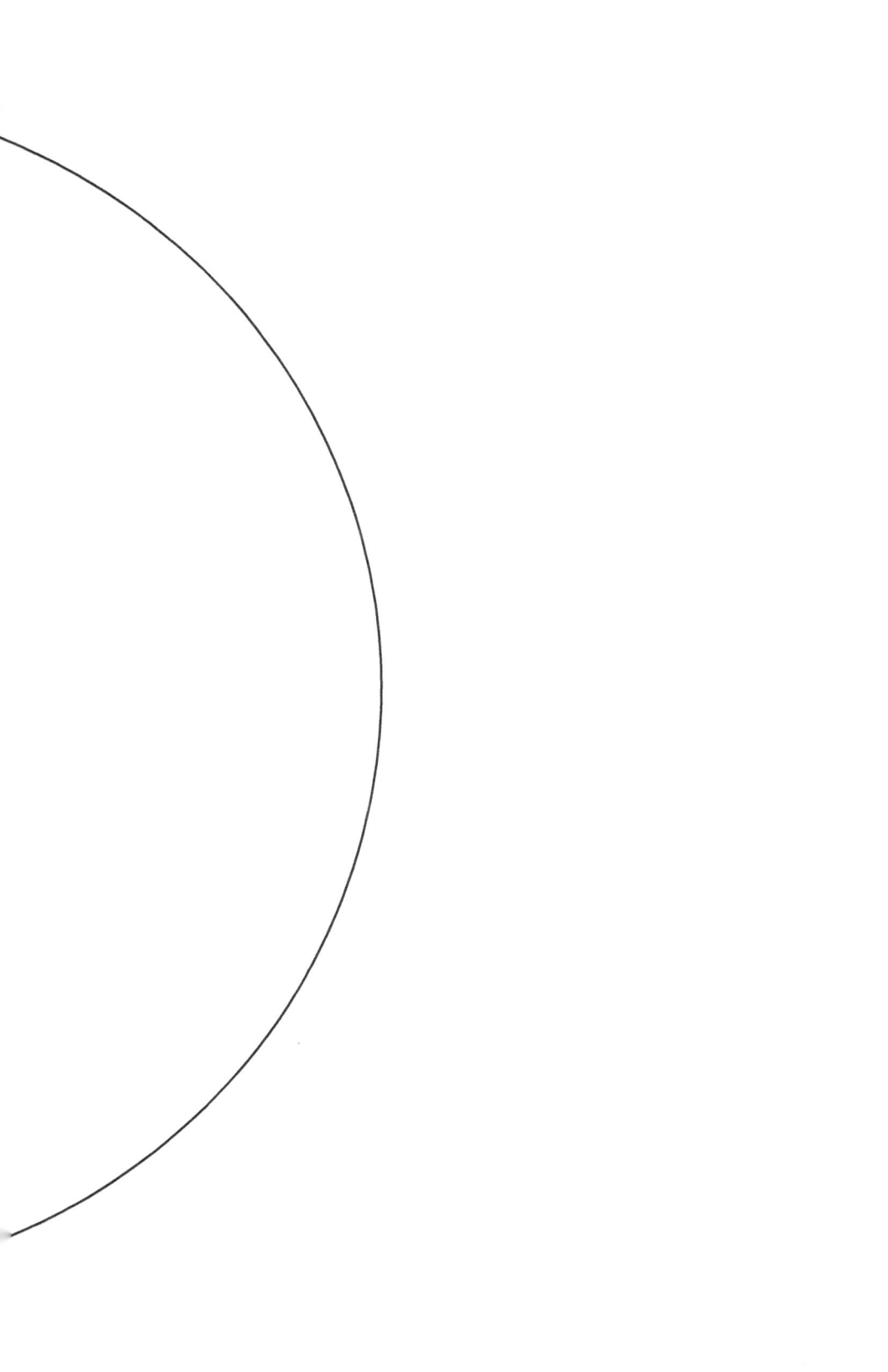

CHAPTER 9

The Timeless Flatulence Proverbs

1. Always rule your Fart. Never allow it to lead you.

2. The man who farts versus the direction of a strong wind gets suffocated by his Fart first.

3. Your character is only defined by how, when, and where you fart.

4. Your Fart is only a fart while it is inside your body. Once you let it out, it is an invisible device to ruin the entire fresh air all around you.

5. The one who releases gas in a closed environment always ends up being exposed to suffocation.

6. Everyone will despise the one who does not know where to start farting constantly.

7. Suppose parents fail to teach their children about the proper

etiquette of releasing gas. They will release massive shame and extreme heartbreak into their future lives.

8. Educate your minor children on where and when to fart. However, be their friends when they are grownups, and they accidentally fart at a party.

9. Suppose you start farting everywhere in confidence without paying any attention to others. Then you have lost your sense of smell.

10. The swinging hands left and right behind the body is an obvious sign of trying desperately to get rid of the fart smell.

11. Early use of the toilet is far better than getting known as the sloppy Farty person.

12. Suppose you try to smell your own gas. All hopes are long gone for you. You are insane already.

13. Show a man a place where to release his gross gas, and you have saved his destiny.

14. The one who passed the Fart is always the one who is trying ridiculously hard to blame others.

15. The gross and highly smelly disasters always come from passing gas carelessly.

16. Suppose you ask about where you can relieve yourself from your gas. You may be an idiot for a few minutes. But if you never ask the question. You will be an idiot for as long as people know you.

17. You always breathe what you have released thru the air.

18. Massive butts fart alike.

19. Not any gross smell in the air is a rotten scent of a fart.

20. The one who tries to stop two farts simultaneously fails miserably in front of others.

21. The one whose hands are firmly covering and pressing a butt will be known as the shameless Farter.

22. A bathroom never used by anyone who is in dire need of passing gas is worthless.

23. You can never excuse yourself and say you were warming up your body if you just passed the gas into the air.

24. Whoever plays with a fart runs a danger of getting into self-suffocation.

25. Never ask: "Who farted?" unless you are positive it was not you in the first place!

26. The one who uses the toilet and counts the farts before they are out of the body will soon get confused.

27. Little attempts can go a long way in preserving the fresh air all around your body.

28. You always get back the smell of what you give away.

29. It is easier to stop releasing your gas than to analyze why you did it and disgrace yourself.

30. A man who farts near a fire must be ready to get burned very seriously. **(Warning: Under NO circumstances, try to flame your Fart!)**

31. An odorless fart is still a fart. (Do not use it as a valid excuse to go and fart around the house.)

32. A man who tries to accept the blame for his wife's accidental farting is genuinely a kind gentleman protecting her reputation.

33. If you are passing gas shamelessly, you are also busy burying your trust, reputation, and better destiny.

34. The one who farts on dates without being sorry ends up being alone forever.

35. He who prefers to hold on to his internal gas is the one who protects fresh air at all costs.

36. The less you release gross gas all around you. The happier people will be with you all the time.

37. Thoughtful people who use any nearby vacant toilets to empty their gas genuinely deserve a medal for preserving fresh air.

38. Think first! Fart second!

39. Never make fun of people who do their best to hold in their farts. You are alive today because of them.

40. The man who farts while riding a bicycle has created a moving farting machine.

41. Never fart while cooking food! Otherwise, people who eat your food would feel like they have just kissed your ass.

42. Personal pride and powerful social status come for those who learn how to master their flatulence skills.

43. The one who forgets to use the toilet right before taking a shower will lose the nose's power while bathing.

44. The one who tries to run after a released fart hoping to catch it and color it later is always considered a loser.

45. You can curse your butt for passing gas at a very wrong time, but you will surely hate anyone who says, "Amen."

46. Farting is never like breathing. Always remember the difference!

47. When it hits the fan, run for your life, or die of suffocation. But, please, don't say I didn't warn you!

48. Teach people how and where to fart, and you have saved their destiny in this world.

49. Your ideal life partner is the one who can secretly build a long-lasting gassy relationship with your Fart.

50. Choose your food wisely, and you will have less shameful gas going out of your body.

51. Small odorless farts are much better than the large gross ones.

52. Finding the closest toilet is always hard before it becomes easy.

53. Never wake up anyone with the loud Kaboom sound of your Fart!

54. It is always hard to forget considerate people who hold on to their farts until they go to the toilet to let it all out.

55. You can never have your Fart out of your body and expect to inhale fresh air nearby. (Unless you are a rare sneaky farter.)

56. You are not picky, judgmental, or superficial. You are just looking for the one who will never judge you when you accidentally fart at a party.

57. You cannot fart and expect it not to land on other people's noses.

58. When it comes to farting, your public shame is not in knowing who did it. It is in asking who did it.

59. Never fall into deep despair! The most disgusting hour is right after a fart has been released into the air. Soon, it will vanish through the air.

60. There will always be fresh, pristine air at the end of the tunnel.

61. An excellent odorless, silent fart is priceless in the market of life.

62. Wise people practice the art of farting properly.

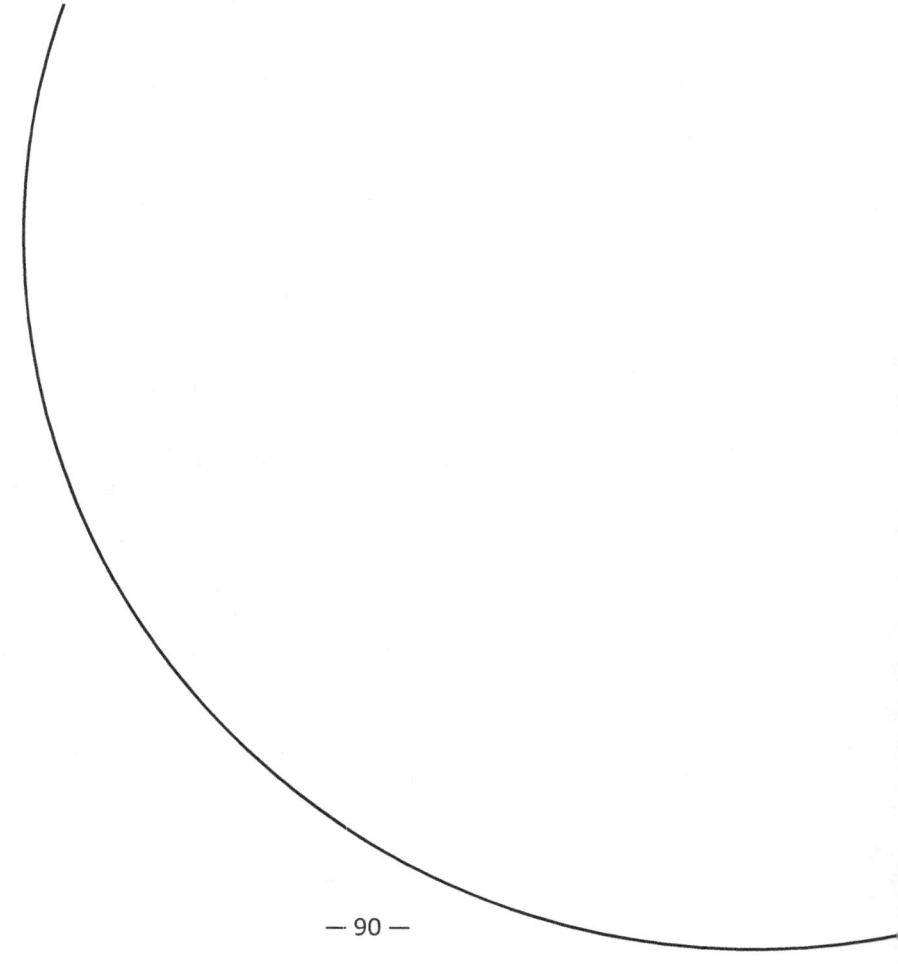

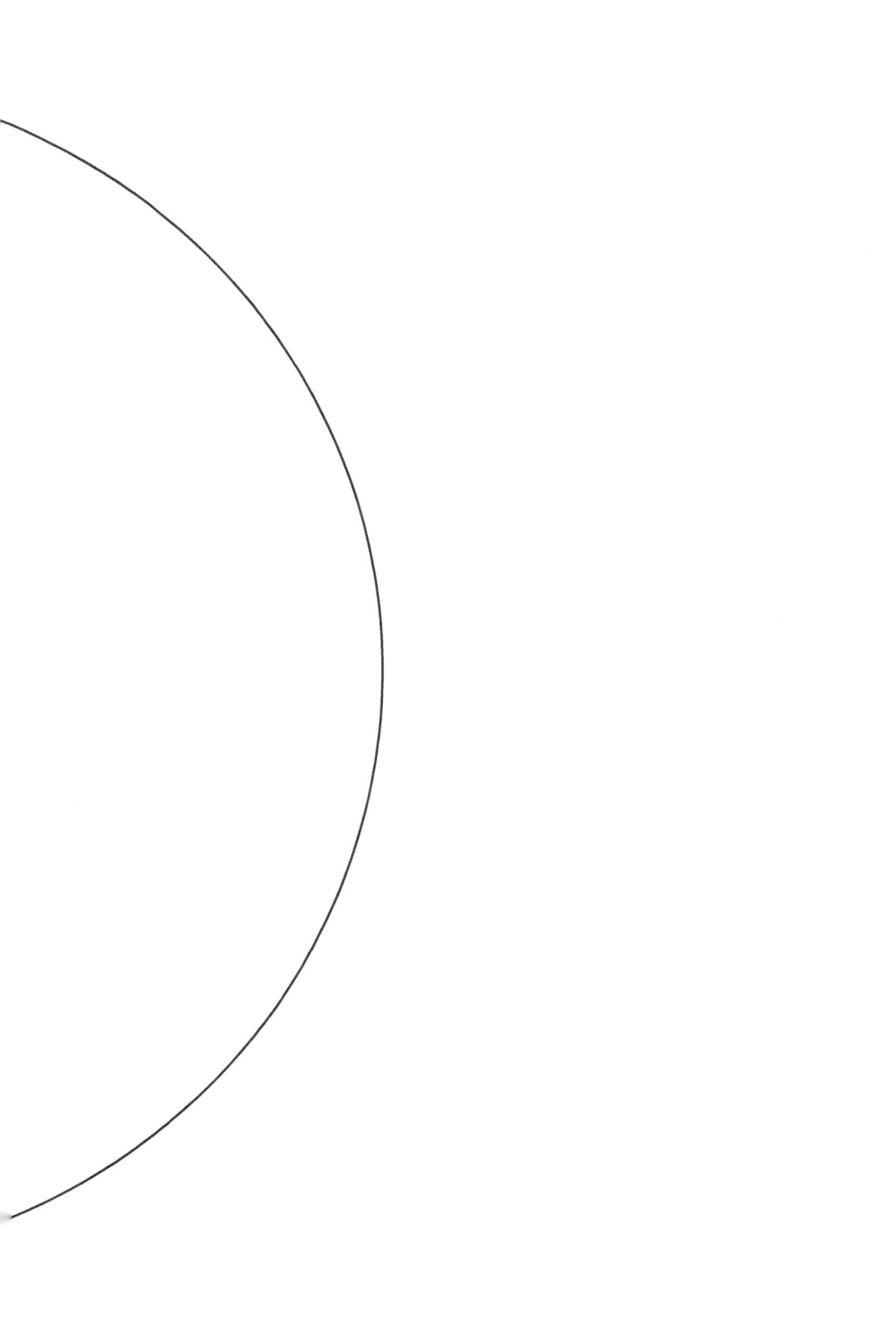

CHAPTER 10

Fartica – A New Hope On The Rise

It Counts When You Care About Your Farting Patients.

Do not despair if your primary care physician has diagnosed you with CFS (Continuous Flatulence Syndrome). There is still hope for you. It is a disease in which the patient keeps releasing the grossest gas in a chain reaction. People suffering from this horrendous disease tend to go for a walk in the parks much more than others. That is because they make sure their loved ones at home (or any closed environments) never get exposed to their farts and die of suffocation.

In recent years, a new pharmaceutical company called: "Green Life" corporation has invented a new effective drug called: Fartica[1].

Medical scientists believe that Fartica[2] is far more effective than simethicone for long-term management and prevention of flatulence

1. This medication does not exist, Nor it is even available to order from any significant Drug Manufacturer. All fictional explanations have been given for entertainment purposes only! Warning: This is an entirely fictitious drug.

2. Since, this medication is an entirely fictitious drug. Therefore, all explanations are in form of dramatizations only.

symptoms. Patients using this drug will have the ability to control the flow, the rate, and the precise time of releasing their farts. It orders the brain to send signals to the nerves on the rectum, and the patients can get a real chance to tighten their external rectum muscles voluntarily. That quickly prevents releasing farts into the air continuously.

Furthermore, depending on your digestive system and metabolism, it changes the foul smell of your Fart into different aromas such as freshly brewed coffee in the morning, a warm ocean breeze, chocolate chip cookies baked in the oven, vanilla ice cream, bacon, and a new all-leather car smell. That brings massive freedom for significantly older adults who are too slow to find the bathroom right away. If they are on Fartica and release some of the most pleasant scents into the air, no one else will ever be upset or angry with them.

In contrast, it works perfectly for pediatric patients, too. The research has shown that most parents are unhappy with their little kids producing good scents while peeing in their diapers. That makes them completely and entirely forget to change their kids' diapers. On the other hand, if you are generally lazy, in the long run, this drug never brings any happiness or freedom of farting for you.

Chances are that other family members or roommates will ask you to prepare, bake, or brew the exact same item as soon as your new scent enters the air. It will create more pain and unnecessary discomfort for all lazy people. For instance, if you are releasing brewed fresh coffee aroma, you will have to get off your lazy bottom and brew a real coffee for others.

Pharmacology Information

Brand Name: Fartica

Generic: Since this is a newly manufactured drug, at this time, there are no therapeutically equivalent generic drugs available.

Route of Administration: Orally: You take it by mouth.

Drug Form: Chewable Tablet (10 mg)

It is only available thru valid and authentic prescriptions. It is not an OTC medication.

Drug Class

Fartica fits into a class of drugs called gastrointestinal agents. They relieve gas in patients experiencing severe bloating and bowel discomforts.

Contraindications

You must avoid consuming this new medication if you have had a history of hypersensitivity or a strong allergic reaction to simethicone or any active ingredients (Aluminum hydroxide and Magnesium hydroxide). This drug is antacid and antigas. Avoid taking other types of OTC Antacid tablets while you are taking Fartica.

Pregnancy Risks

It has a pregnancy category X. DO NOT take this medication while pregnant. Inform your doctor about your pregnancy. Never keep it as a personal secret if you have taken it accidentally. Chances are your unborn baby may come out along with your fart out of the wrong exit way sooner than your biological standard delivery time.

Although it is not excreted into breast milk, talk to your doctor if you are breastfeeding. Take extreme caution for all nursing women. Taking this drug while breastfeeding can have severe reverse side effects in healthy infants. After all, you never want to create little farters running around your home for the upcoming years.

Side Effects & Adverse Reactions

Bear in mind this new medication must never be used for any other types of gastrointestinal diseases.

Currently, FDA (Flatulence Development Association) has not finished the official approval process for this new drug.

Drug-To-drug Interaction

Simethicone: Risk X: Avoid taking simultaneously!

Omeprazole: Avoid Combination!

Famotidine: Risk X: Avoid Combination, or you will turn into a lean, mean disgusting farting machine.

About Green Life Corporation

We are the world-class supplier of nearly all comprehensive Flatulence-related medication developments. As a company that has been in the pharmaceutical industry for a long time, we know how important it is to prescribe the effective proper medication at the right time for all your patients.

We are determined to solve all your farting problems through application and creating the best, most effective, and most economical drugs. Many of our employees are also diagnosed with CFS. At this point, we decided to make a specific potent drug to treat our sick employees. We need to breathe at work, too. We made our decision that enough was enough. That was why we created a consistent stand against CFS disease.

We constantly feel suffocated while we are working with others. Imagine the fatal effects of hundreds of farts going into your office air all at the same time. We had to create a new effective drug for our employees. It was more a matter of life and death for us. Then, we all decided to place it on our worldwide production line.

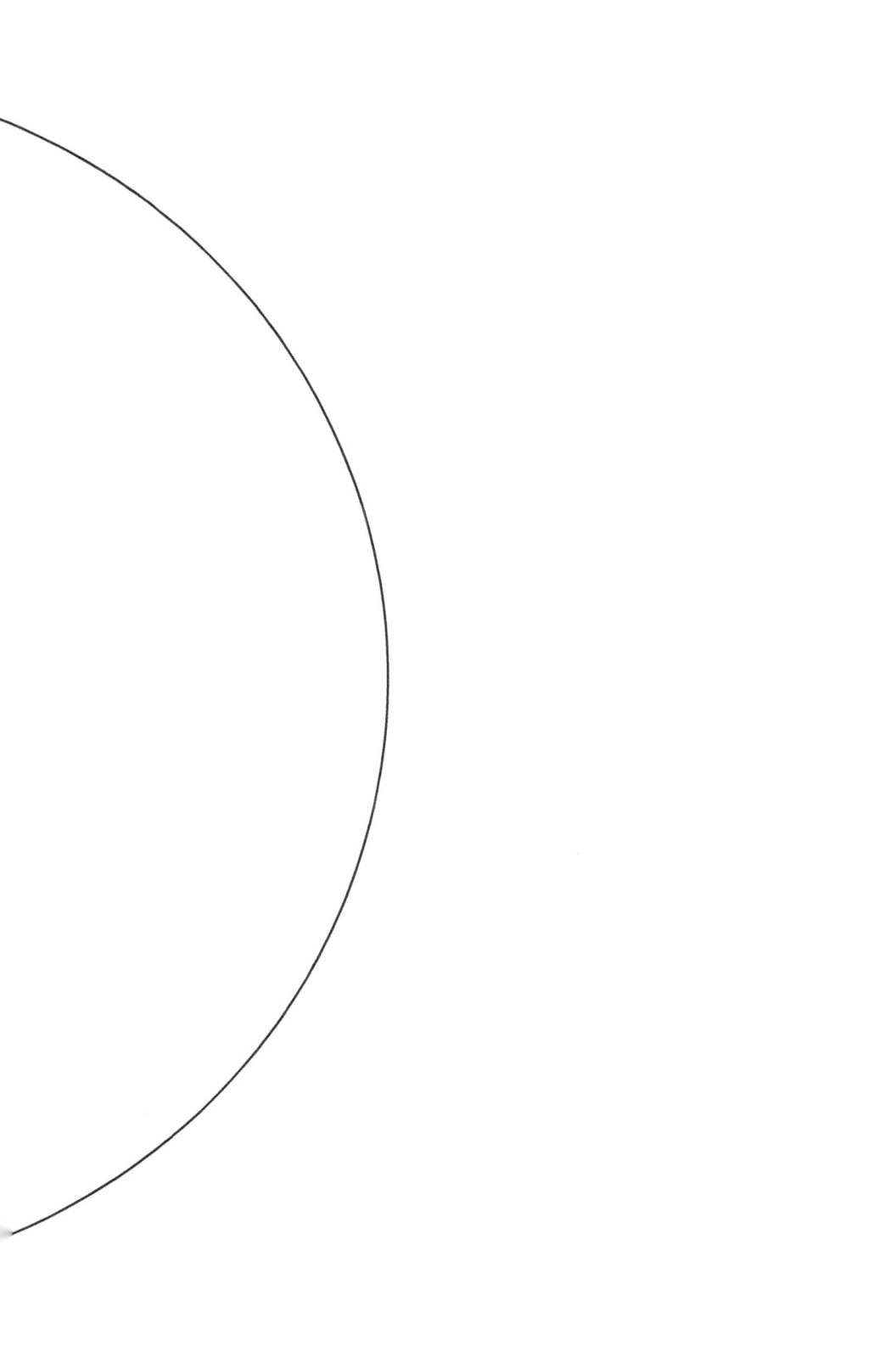

CHAPTER 11

The Symbolic Usage of A Fart On TV

The Most Farting Man in the World

Years ago, he farted his ass off in the public bathroom. He farted so loudly that people thought his ass was exploding. He wanted to try farting under the water. So, he went swimming in the local lake. He farted under the water and killed so many lake monsters. When aliens abducted him, he farted on their faces over and over again. They were aware their technology was no match for his stinky human gas. They released him right away and never returned to earth for the next twenty years. If he were to give you directions on having the smelliest human gas, you would have to eat many expired eggs. Then you would have to live practically in a cave in a general solitude state.

His smelly gassy legend proceeds him, the way urine works side by side of the pee.

He has the largest database of most rotten gasses in his ass. And it is said he has never tried to release them one by one. He knew the liability of being a mass murderer in the eyes of the justice system. When he decides to send you his Fart right away, he will go to the rooftop and Fart in the direction of the wind. You could never get away from his gas.

When there is a stinky thunderstorm, it is because he is breaking powerful winds everywhere. His Fart smells like a biological weapon.

He once lost consciousness only to notice that he was farting in his sleep two days later while failing to leave his bedroom windows open.

He is the most farting man in the world.

I don't often break smelly gas in public, but when I do. I make sure I eat lots of cooked rotten cow's meat for breakfast. Stay gassy, my friend!

"It's Only Your Own Fart." Commercial

It is not a donkey's fart.

It is not a monkey's fart.

It is not an alien's fart.

It is not your urine. It

is not even your pee.

It's Only Your Own Fart.

Introducing the Fart Buster 5000 kit

Got a neighbor who always farts around his house and makes your whole place stink, too?

Or you have few family members who always carry around an endless supply of the grossest farts inside their bodies?

Are you hosting a large barbecue party, and unidentified sneaky farters are going around and are just making the day too gross to handle for everyone?

Don't worry! Your struggles and frustrations are over now.

You need to get the Fart Buster 5000 kit.

- It is equipped to disperse the most pleasant odors into the air for the next five days in a row.

- It also has a farting radar detector[1] that pinpoints all the crafty unknown farters and shows you their exact location all over the map of your house.

- Fart Buster 5000 also sends automatic warning text messages to all careless farters in your party. It politely asks them to stop farting around, or the host or the hostess will kick them out of the party.

- If the text messages wouldn't stop the farters. Then, it will announce their names loudly.

- It also has detailed recipes of all fart-free food and ingredients available at your fingertips. The recipes are precisely tailored to your family members' age and unique metabolism.

- You can connect it to any wall outlet.

- It comes with a solar battery panel and rechargeable batteries, too. Once you charge them on a sunny day or with electric power. It will work for ten days.

- It is an energy-efficient unit and saves you lots of money on your power bill.

- Call the number on your screen now! Order today, and we drop $50 off of the $500.00 total price of your new Fart Buster 5000.

---

1. Customers must press the yellow-colored "Fart-Sampling" button on the back of the unit to activate this feature. Unfortunately, at this time, this feature only works if you have already sampled all your guests' farts using your unit.

- Fart Buster 5000 also comes with advanced Bluetooth and wireless capabilities. After you connect it to your wireless network, it automatically gets connected to the International Fart Registry of WFO[2].

- During this TV promotion, if you register the scent of your Fart with WFO, you'll receive another $50.00 farting registration discount. Just activate the wireless feature on your unit and fart into the sampling funnel section. Close the lid and wait for 5 minutes! The kit will automatically analyze and register your unique fart and enters all your info into the International Fart Registry of WFO.

- If you choose to sign up and pay an extra monthly fee of $49.99, you can even recharge your Fart Buster 5000 batteries using your unique Farts[3].

- Enjoy[4] having the unique power to get rid of all gross human gas in your home once and for all.

Here is how to get your $50.00 Discount

- Just make sure you post us a copy of your sealed and dated registration slip by Registered Mail in the next two weeks. You

---

2. WFO (World Flatulence Organization)

3. Offer is valid for new and qualifying former customers only! Certain farting credit requirements apply! You must present valid and recent paperwork from WFO (World Flatulence Organization) stating and proving that you have not been traveling around and emptying your gross gas into the air all around the globe during the past three years. A minimum of a 5-year contract is required. There are no cancellation fees during the first 90 days of your new service. However, if you miss the 90-day deadline, you will forfeit your right to receive any refund. After that, all gassy-related sales are final. Remember that there are no refunds after the first 90 days of the service, even if you run after your fart, catch it, color it, let it be air-dried, and mail it to us!

All farting requirements are subject to change without further notice!

4. We have not been successful in selling more than 2000 units worldwide. In the beginning, we were outraged with all those know-it-all folks. However, we did let it slide. (Thanks to all you smarty-pants out there who learned how, when, and where you must fart. Overall, it is what it is.).

can connect your unit to any wireless printer and print it in no time.

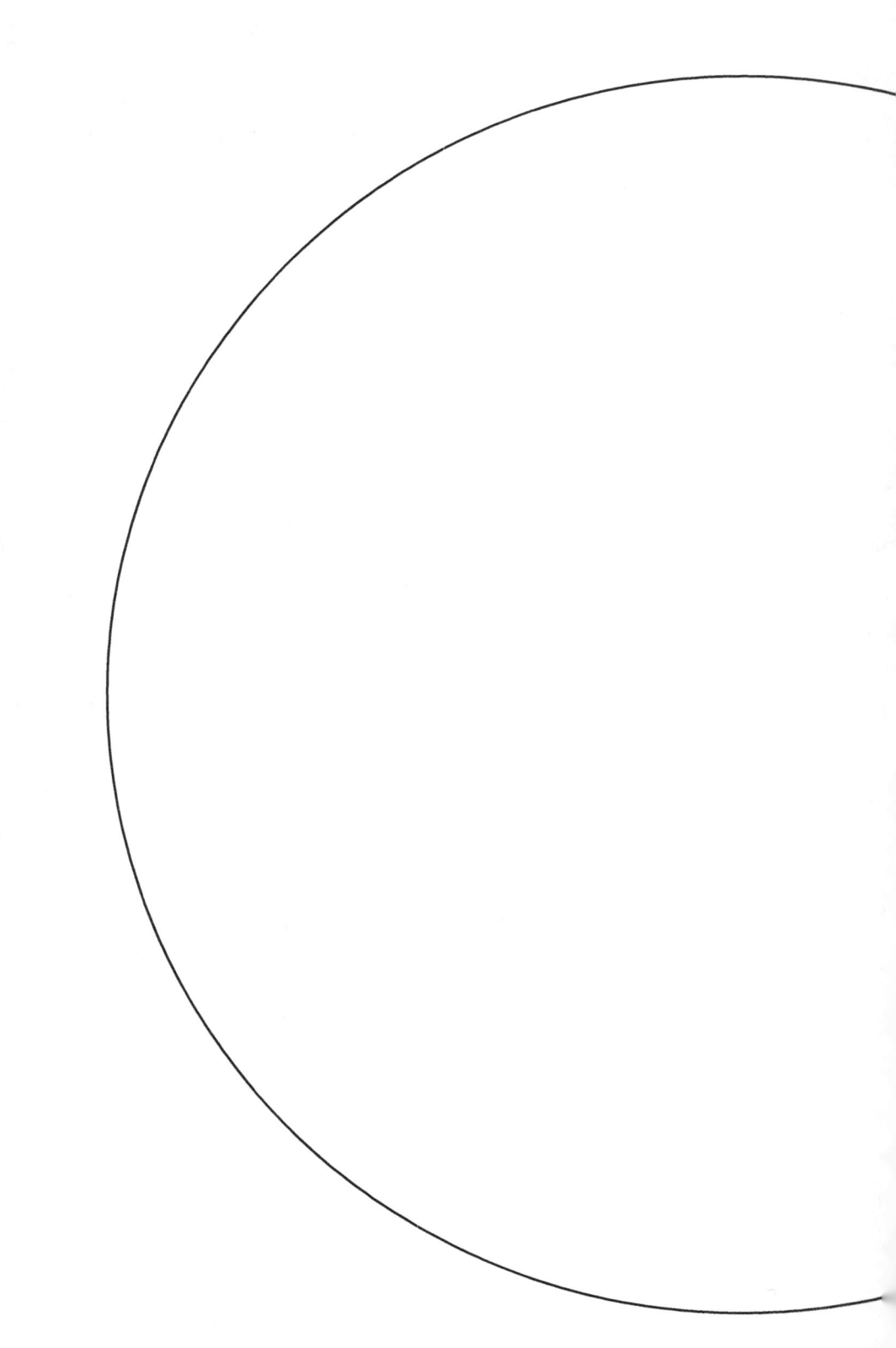

CHAPTER 12

The Hilarious Fart Jokes

How can you tell when a housefly is farting in the air? If you notice, it is flying in a straight line.

Why don't rich people never have to fart into their wallets? Because they don't need it. They already have enough gas money.

Why don't the geologists never talk about dinosaurs' farts? Because they are the blasts from the past.

Healthwise, your fart should always weigh zero. If not, then you are dealing with much more severe problems.

Why do most countries allow royal families to fart in public? Because Noble gas is considered nonreactive everywhere in the world.

Why do we consider the farts the best super spies in the world of espionage? Since nobody can ever see them. They can be very silent and deadly everywhere they go during their highly classified secret missions.

Why is it the worst idea to fart in a moving elevator? Because then you will be wrong on many various levels.

Do you know why most farters fantasize about living on the Uranus planet? Because Uranus produces hydrogen sulfide, a gas that smells like their gross farts. Hence, it is their ideal exotic paradise. And if they live there, no one can ever find out who did it in the first place.

What is the most challenging task in the world other than working in the mine? It is holding in your fart on your days off when you are all alone at home.

How can you be sure you have just had a brain fart? If you are brilliant and have just come up with the worst idea.

Why does God never allow any ghost to fart in the afterlife? Because everyone hates the spirit bomb.

In the animal kingdom, what is entirely invisible and has a fresh steak smell in the air? The Supreme Fart of an Eagle.

Why do all the horses release gas when they are about to jump? Because a horse's biological engine works exactly like the engine of a car. It can never reach optimum horsepower without burning any gas.

You are never the only one who is suffering from a hard life. Let us think about all the chairs in the movie theaters, restaurants, stadiums, park benches, airplane seats, and your sofa at home! They are the ones who have had it the worst since their invention. They are all silently and patiently tolerating the pain of dealing with a massive number of farts daily.

What do success and a fart have in common? People always hate them both equally since they only come from others.

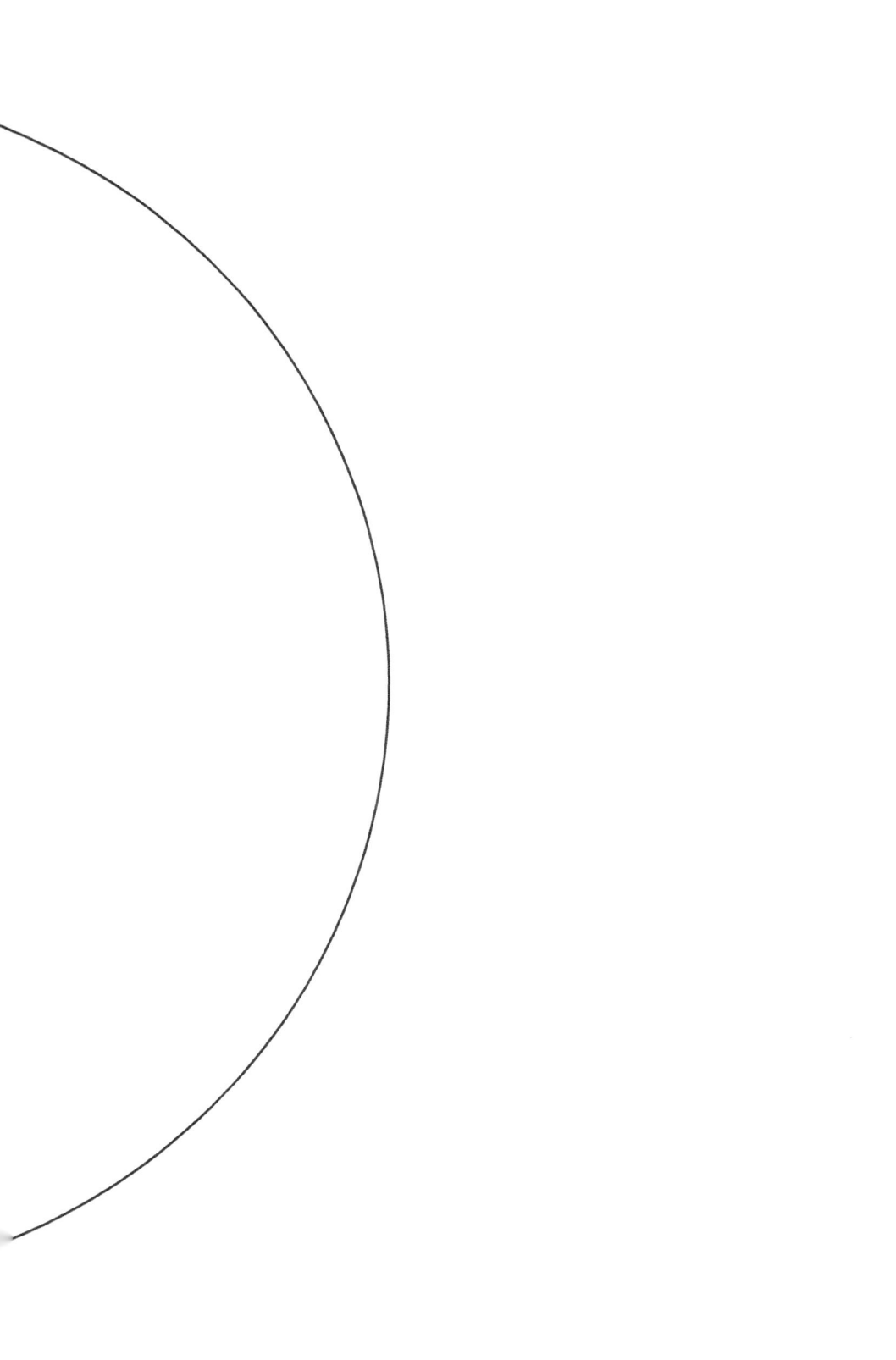

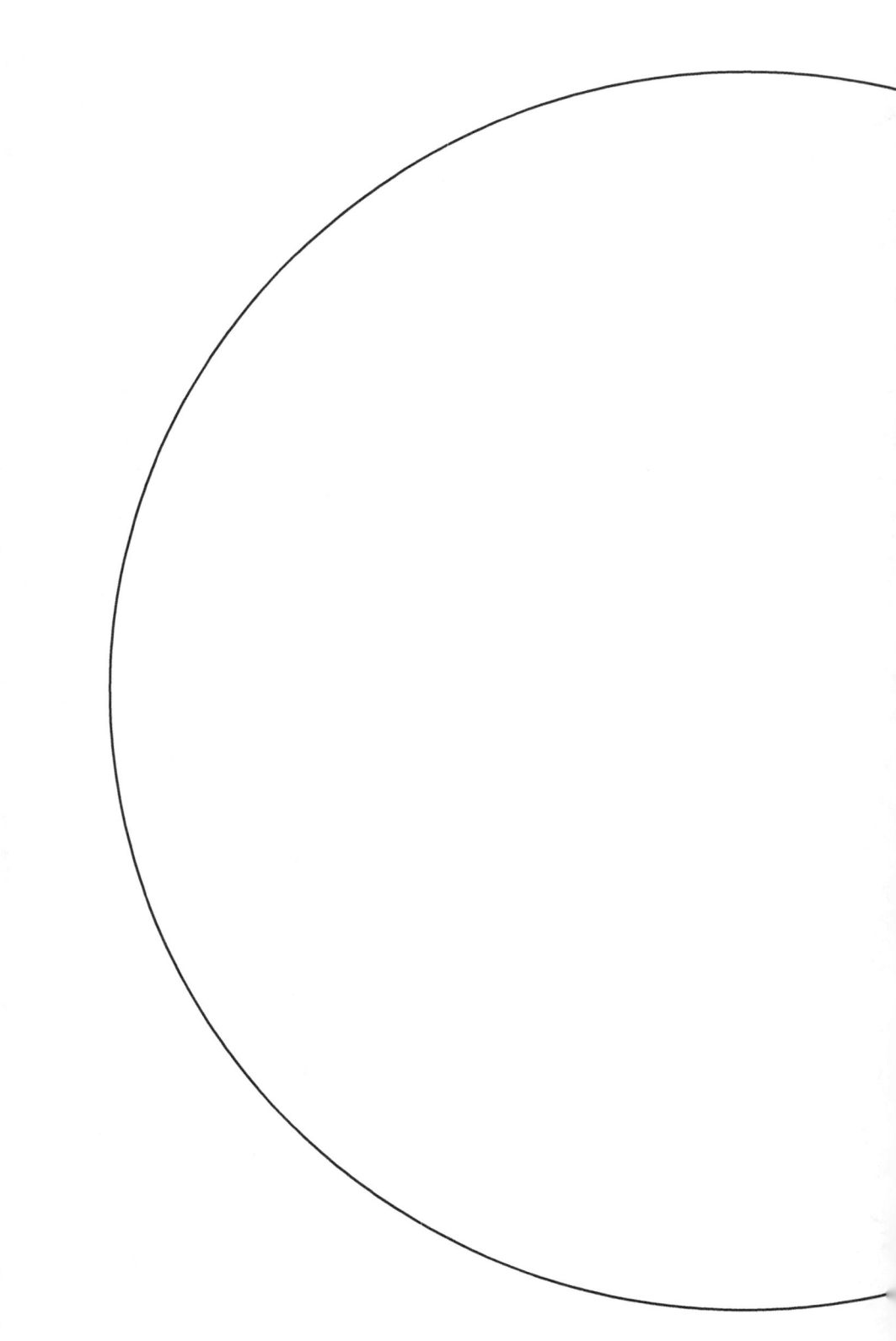

CHAPTER 13

The Conclusion

Now I would like to stop your reading and draw your attention to all you have learned. Join me to celebrate one of your most productive victories against your gross bodily gas.

By now, you surely know about one of the most basic gassy functions of your body. You currently have the knowledge, wisdom, and deep understanding of controlling it from going out of your body anytime and anywhere.

You are also well aware of this undeniable fact. No matter how hard your fart is desperately trying to go into the air all around you, you already have the necessary will, skills set, tools, and your trained brain. Thus, you allow it to happen only during the most appropriate times. You feel comfort and peace of mind.

You have come a long way to learn, study, and improve all your fart-related skills and social activities. Most of your shame and becoming a laughingstock in any social gathering always goes back to a single act of involuntarily farting among the crowd.

In the long run you will see how reading this book has assisted you in becoming one of the best artists in the timeless art of farting. In time, you indeed have turned into an individual who instantly commands respect, public appreciation, timely attention, and general care.

People will notice your practical farting skills everywhere you go. Without reading this remarkable book, none of those fascinating gifts would have entered your life.

May your long journey of life always be free from all unwanted farts.

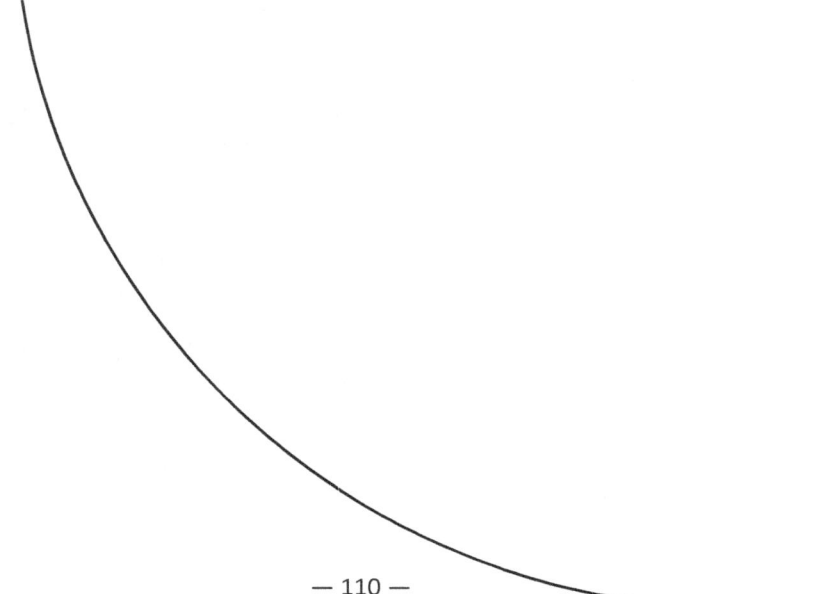

Flatulence Vocabulary & Acronyms

AFAP: American Fresh Air Preservation, this international medical academy was initially built by Dr. B.A (Big Ass) Fartin. (Refers to Chapter Five: Introducing the All-New Fart Clinic)

CFS: Continuous Flatulence Syndrome (Not an actual disease) It is a disease in which the patient keeps releasing the grossest gas in a chain reaction. (Refers to Chapter Ten: Fartica)

CSA: Chief Smelling Agent: Refers to Chapter Four: The Elusive Farterella

FDA: Flatulence Development Association (Not an actual FDA organization)

Fart: noun: (or flatus) intestinal gas produced by your digestive system. Verb: the act of releasing gas out of the body and into the world

Farter : subject: someone or an animal that releases gas through the anus or simply farts.**(Farter: singular form, Farters: Plural form)**

Fartica: the new latest drug to treat CFS (Continuous Flatulence Syndrome) made by the Green Life Pharmaceutical (Not an actual

Drug, dramatization)

Fartista: (noun) This vast land has been the founding home to the world's oldest farters, including Alexander, Napoleon, Hitler, Genghis Khan, and Alcibiades.

Farty: adjective: displaying the gross characteristic of a fart

Gooz: (pronounced as a goose in English) Persian word for a loud fart (noun)(also the word "Choss," which the Persians widely use this slang word for a silent fart. It refers to Chapter Six: The Untold Ancient Truth Behind Jacuzzi.)

Goozoo: Persian word for a Farter (subject) refers to Chapter Six.

UWS: Underground Windbreaker Society (refers to Chapter One.)

WFO: World Flatulence Organization

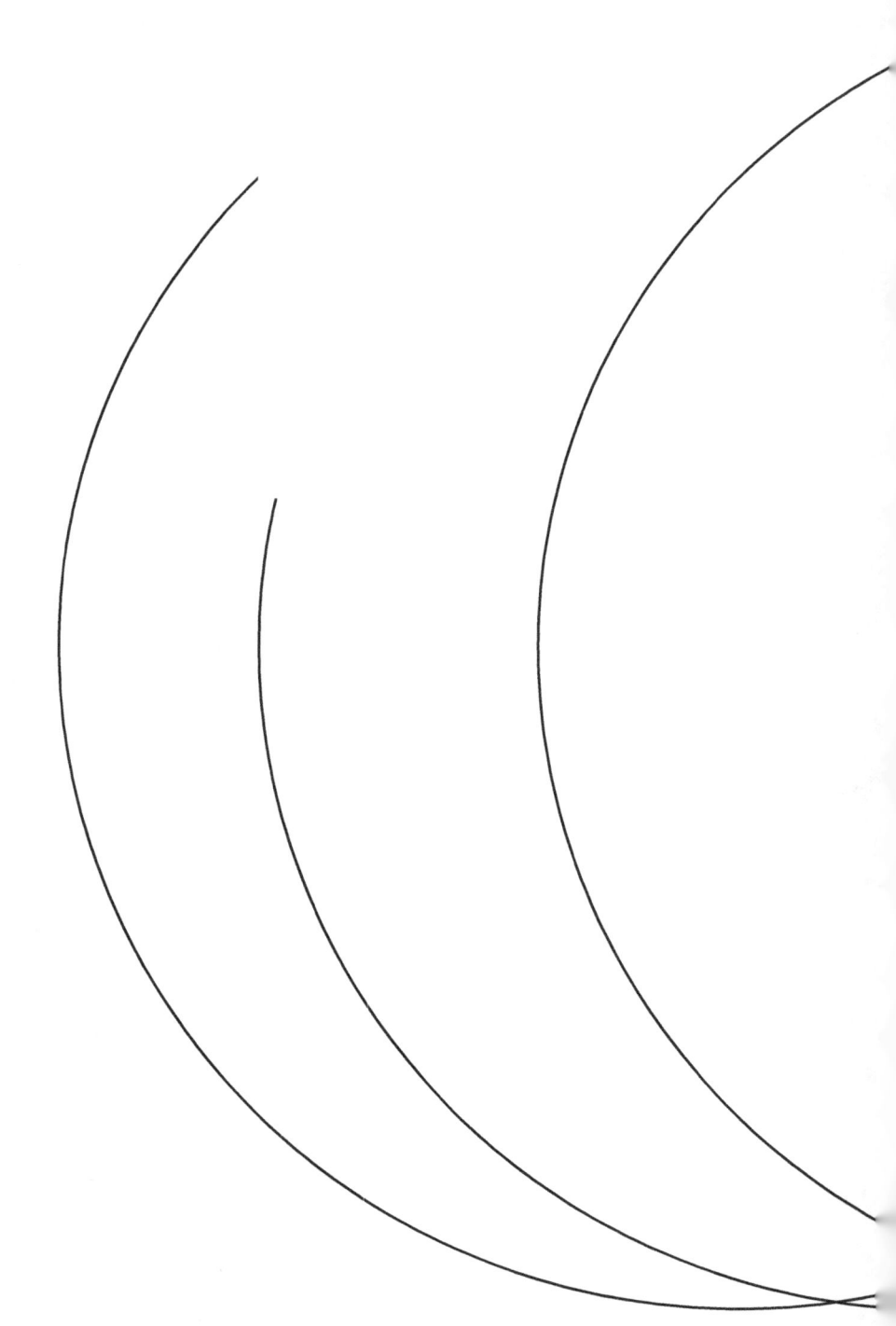

ABOUT THE AUTHOR

Parviz Shirmohammadi is a multi-talented aspiring writer. This is his first published book. His writing brings the most delightful reading experience for all readers worldwide. In his free time, he likes reading, playing chess, and learning about creative writing tasks. Overall, English writing has always been one of his passions in life. He has romantic poetries, and books in other genres, too.

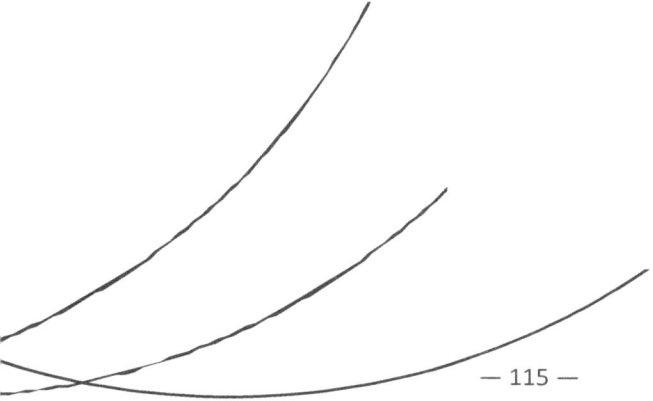